EIRIN THOMPSON

The Undercover Mother

HACHETTE
BOOKS
IRELAND

First published in 2008 by Hachette Books Ireland
A division of Hachette Livre UK Ltd.
First published in paperback in 2008

1

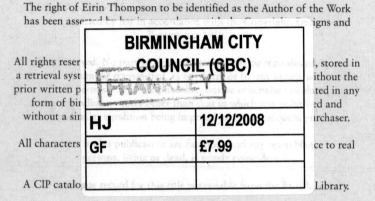
ISBN 978 0 340 95085 2

Typeset in Sabon by Hachette Books Ireland
Printed and bound in the UK by CPI Mackays, Chatham ME5 8TD

Hachette Books Ireland policy is to use papers that are natural, renewable
and recyclable products and made from wood grown in sustainable forests.
The logging and manufacturing processes are expected to conform to the
environmental regulations of the country of origin.

Hachette Books Ireland
8 Castlecourt Centre
Castleknock
Dublin 15, Ireland
A division of Hachette Livre UK Ltd.
338 Euston Road, London NW1 3BH

www.hbgi.ie

For Niall

Part One

Water in the Electrics

I really want this job.

*

Actually, I really need this job.

*

My elderly friends Kathleen and Lorna have so got into being Happy Grannies. Ever since they were paired up with Fiona, Simon and their two little sons, Nathan and Samuel, they're busy all the time. They've stopped meeting me for milky coffees in Mumbles restaurant because of its lack of a comprehensive no-smoking policy and instead bring the boys to the brand new and completely smoke-free Tasty Ranch, which has opened beside the also relatively recent Riverside shopping mall. I've seen them through the window, in their complimentary paper cowboy hats, eating their chargrilled burgers. The only coffee the TR does is the watery black kind in paper cups with add-your-own fake milk portions.

I support the Happy Grannies scheme in principle. In an era when young families and grandparents often live many miles apart, it enables people to hook up with a substitute missing-half-of-their-equation in their own area. It even takes on people like Kathleen and Lorna, who don't have any grandchildren of their own but would like to. I could have done with some of that when our children were very young and Eleanor and Terry, my parents, were far away.

Sometimes Lorna plays with Nathan and Samuel while Kathleen does Fiona and Simon's ironing, and they go round to help Simon – i.e., to give Fiona peace of mind – while Fiona goes to aquarobics on Monday evening, and they babysit the boys on some Saturday nights so that Fiona and Simon can go out together to the cinema/theatre/pub/ restaurant. And the whole thing is free of charge, because Happy Grannies is a voluntary scheme, which is supposed to reward the otherwise-redundant oldies with fulfilling new relationships and meaningful endeavour.

Simon, Fiona, Nathan and Samuel call my friends 'Granny Kathleen' and 'Granny Lorna'. I call Simon and Fiona 'jammy', because I'm completely uncharitable and probably more than a bit jealous. Anyhow, now that Kathleen and Lorna have their new family, I hardly see them.

It was a big blow when the Listening Angels' thrift shop shut, and all the harder because it happened so suddenly that our little team was thrown to the four winds. The investigative documentary *Listening Angels? Listen to This!* went out on a Tuesday night, and on the Wednesday morning our area manager, Mrs Nilsson, rang, telling us to shut up shop and go home until further notice. Of course, we didn't go home, we went to Mumbles and discussed the situation, and it felt like the whole town was queuing up to talk to us, as if we were celebrities for the day, because it was such a big scandal and everyone wanted to know the inside story. But we didn't know the inside story.

Everyone knows that the Listening Angels Trust was set up by a woman whose daughter killed herself because she'd no one to talk to, but we were as shocked as anyone to discover that our founder had not merely been flying herself to America for fundraising purposes but also to spend a week in Disneyland with her partner, his son and the son's family on the Angels' Visa card. She'd also moved into a country house with a pool and an all-weather tennis court and started driving a Porsche 911. It was hard to see who was going to buy Christmas cards, fridge memo boards and second-hand clothes from us now that it looked like the profits were being siphoned into that woman's pocket. All the people who had been bringing us their old garments and bric-a-brac because we were on a side street with easy vehicle access, would probably revert to double-parking on the high street while they bundled their stuff into Oxfam.

I suppose it was worst for Margaret, our shop manager.

She was the one among us who was on a wage for her work. When it became clear that the Angels had died a swift and irreversible death, she was fuming – even though it was common knowledge in the shop that she'd long been hoping to move across town to Save the Children. She's working in a call centre, now, but I don't think it'll suit her as well as the Angels' shop, when she used to disappear on supposed training days and Kathleen, Lorna and I covered her arse because we actually liked it better when she wasn't there.

We also lost our resident male, the lovely Seamus Kelly. Seamus was an IT wizard and bodhrán enthusiast who took a gap year to come and work with us in our drop-in facility. He hadn't been in place six months before the furore occurred and now he's finishing off his time out learning how to weave tweed somewhere in Donegal.

I still have my Fridays in the market, helping former special-needs teacher Marilyn Softly on her environmentally friendly stall, but I don't think she really likes me. I was merely the only unemployed person she knew when she was getting up and running, plus I'm pretty good at counting in my head, which Marilyn is not. And, anyhow, I don't think she can be making much money at the stall: first there was the palaver with all the zips sticking on the Fair Trade hoodies, and then the stripy rainbow jackets ran into themselves in the wash and had to be refunded, and it also turned out that not as many people as Marilyn had anticipated wanted to buy biodegradable cornstarch bin

liners when they could just as easily use their old
supermarket bags for nothing. We sell a lot of recycled-
vending-cup pencils, but not sufficient, I fear, to provide one
proprietor and an assistant with a wage. I think if Marilyn
felt she could trust one of the other stall-holders to keep an
eye on her pitch while she took her toilet breaks, I'd be out
on my ear.

Jill, on the other hand, my neighbour in the avenue
where we live (and whose electioneering husband was last
year the subject of a homosexual sex scandal) is thriving! Her
modern 'inset' shop, Jill's, now occupies as much space in her
husband Trevor's formerly old-fashioned shoe emporium as
his leather brogues, black school shoes and zip-up slippers.
Unfortunately I'm not groomed enough to seek a job from
swish Jill, who is perpetually tanned and glamorously shod in
shoes from her own stock. I definitely fit in better with the
fingerless-gloved Fagin types at the market.

Meanwhile, I'm also missing Lucy, my next-door
neighbour and sometime counsellor. She's had another little
turn and her husband Tom is afraid she'll induce a second
brain injury if she has any stress, so I've been politely banned
from talking to her about my problems.

So, you see, with everybody amputated from my life in one
way or another, I really need this job for someone to talk to.

Despite (or perhaps because of) the upheaval, I'm still
on pretty good terms with *him*, but he has been working
extra hours, which means I only get to see him in the weary

little strip of time before bed when we're both past wanting to talk and prefer to veg out in front of a crime drama. That's another reason why I must get this job: so he won't have to work extra hours.

Something that has not departed from my life, and probably never will, is, of course, the endless bloody house-work, which, like the poor, will always be with us, and never seems to come anywhere near to completion.

And by the way, why is the easy way to put a double duvet into a duvet cover harder than the hard way?

* * *

Once again, I had forgotten that yesterday was News Day for year two, so our youngest child had nothing worthwhile to report because we had failed to provide him with any stimulating experiences at the weekend. For his news, he told the class that he'd had a Kit-Kat for breakfast. We had run out of Frosties. Grrrreat. This weekend we must find a forest park/agricultural show/vintage car rally/craft workshop to bring him to. We must also buy him a box of the sawdustiest, raisiniest muesli we can find. He has brought this on himself.

*

Last night's crime drama was brilliant. It was my favourite, featuring maverick cop Jamie 'Mac' McDonald. Of course, all TV cops are maverick – except Detective Inspector Bill Worthington, who only presides over middle-class, bloodless murders in picturesque villages, the grit of his job is represented by him missing supper with his sainted wife – but Mac is yet more maverick than most. Even his good looks are original in a TV world of dark and handsome or blond and handsome: Mac is a flame-haired Celt with jutting cheekbones and eyes you'd love to meet. He's an insomniac who reads Coleridge into the night, and the only person who calls him 'Jamie' is the sweet ex-wife with whom you suspect he's still a little bit in love.

Except Mac doesn't have time for love and marriage. He has cases to solve and nutters to fathom and track down, if he's to protect the public from further acts of carnage as only he can. Naturally he's surrounded by mediocrity – superior officers who lack his gut instincts about the villains, and junior colleagues who are fed up doing the donkey work in pursuit of Mac's seemingly incredible hunches (even though last week Mac's incredible hunch led them directly to the killer, and the week before that, and the week before that). Last night's episode was the first of a two-parter so I still have the second half to look forward to.

*

Aaagh! Playground parent! Was this the morning I was supposed to be on duty? Quick, quick! Diary, diary!

*

Panic averted over playground-parent duty. I'm not on until tomorrow. This is a new scheme introduced by the Parents' Committee to try to combat the morning-traffic mayhem.

Until recently, all children had to be dropped off in the ten-minute window before the start of school because there were no teachers to supervise them any earlier; running around alone was deemed unsafe and, perhaps more inarguably, uninsurable. Consequently there were almost punch-ups every morning as everybody arrived at school at the same time and parked along both sides of the access road round the school gates. Women drivers were afraid to ease their cars on to the constricted roadway and men took to driving on the pavement. And when I say there were almost punch-ups, I really mean it. More importantly, it was only a matter of time before a child was knocked down or run over because all the drivers were so preoccupied with the other cars that they had stopped seeing the children. Somebody had to do something.

That somebody turned out to be Caroline, secretary of the Parents' Committee, who had the presence of mind to bring a clipboard and pad to school one morning while the mayhem was happening and collect the names of parents willing to take turns at supervising the playground from eight thirty till nine. That way, all the mad traffic would be thinned out over half an hour. Unprecedented numbers said yes. Crafty Caroline now has their details when it comes to seeking help with the Bingo Night/Fun Day/Apple Supper. Hence the playground-parent scheme. Those of us participating all had to have police checks and the cost of that means we now need a Quiz Night to replenish our Parents' Committee funds.

*

Experience? I definitely won't get this job if I don't hurry up and do something about filling in the application form. But experience? After being alive, even just hanging around doing very little for all these years, I know a thing or two. But is any of it likely to impress an appointment panel? I mean, I know that 'Adeste Fideles' is just Latin for 'O Come, All Ye Faithful'; I know that a small child can go tobogganing quite successfully in a roasting tin; I know that anxiety will always go away eventually (even if it must, sooner or later, return), but who cares about any of that? They must mean 'relevant experience', mustn't they? In which case, I seem to have none at all.

* * *

In a moment of madness I put companionship with him ahead of my love affair with Jamie 'Mac' McDonald. Instead of watching the second and concluding episode at the time of broadcast, I taped it so that we could watch it together when he finally got home after working his extra hours. Except it turns out I didn't tape it, or the video recorder has broken down. Now I'll never know how it worked out in the end! This is what happens when you try to be nice.

*

Today I took the car through the hot-foam car-wash. It was quite relaxing, even sitting in the queue watching the cars ahead being scrubbed and hosed. I'd like to take the car through the car-wash every week, instead of waiting until strangers have written rude messages in the grime with their fingers, but it costs £4 a time. Yet another reminder of the need to get my job application posted off. I'm down to the section on references. I do not want to ask Margaret, my ex-manager at the thrift shop, because (a) she's mean-spirited and would be bound to give me a mean reference, and (b) I don't think she's all that bright, and her poor skills might reflect badly on me. Could I ask Mrs Nilsson, our goddess-like area manager? But how would I find her?

*

There are only two Nilssons in the phone book. This is promising, providing Mrs Nilsson is not ex-directory.

*

Mrs Nilsson is ex-directory.

*

There's a DJ on Zero FM who likes to think he can find anything for anyone. Marilyn keeps the radio tuned to Zero FM behind the market stall and I've heard him find lots of things for people, like lost dogs and recordings of 'Count' John McCormack. Could he find me a tape of last night's episode of *Mac*? Would I have to go on air, if I phoned in, and give my actual name? Or could they just read out the problem from a card? I must act quickly before whoever has it tapes over it.

* * *

In our local paper, I've found a suitably interesting event for us to attend this weekend: a Family Activity Day at the Millennium Exhibition and Arts Centre. That should show year two the sort of people they're dealing with.

* * *

Marilyn has agreed to give me a reference. I think this is on the understanding that it's a farewell gift; she's had enough of me watching over the demise of her funky ethical market stall. I need to get this job more than ever now, if Marilyn is laying me off.

*

My request for the *Mac* video was read out this morning, along with a lot of nonsense about why women cannot parallel park, fold maps or work video recorders. This is the price you pay for going public: you are held up to ridicule.

* * *

What am I supposed to do with all the crap we produced at the Family Activity Day? It's fine the tutors encouraging the children to glue lots of things together and explore contrasting textures but we now have three tower blocks of toilet-roll tubes, rags, bits of old doily and egg box. I admit that the children had fun making them, but did we have to bring them home? What are we expected to do with them? This is where I wish I could get an honest look into other people's lives: truthfully, do they keep these creations? And if so, for how long? Where do they put them? Or do they chuck them straight in the bin?

*

A girl rang from Zero FM to say that a man has the *Mac* video for me; he will send it to them and they'll send it to me. She said I don't need to worry about reimbursing him for the postage because they'll send him a station goodie-bag to a much greater value than the stamps. She said she wouldn't be sending me a goodie-bag because on this occasion I was already the beneficiary of the transaction and also because they're running out of bubble-wrap.

*

There's not going to be a new *Mac* mystery tonight because we're having another week-long TV 'spectacular'. This one is called *The North, East, West, South Talent Show* and it's going to be on every night at eight up to and including Sunday. It is called *The North, East, West, South Talent Show* because all the contestants are NEWS-readers. The *Radio Times* carries an attractive picture of Anna Ford playing her acoustic guitar in the 1960s but she doesn't even feature in this competition and the written text says it hopes the 'Talent' will be provided with decent microphones to drown the sound of barrels being scraped.

*

Oh, for goodness' sake. On News Day he told year two he drew an alien. Which he did, of course, last night, with an old biro on the back of a bit of brown envelope. But what sort of news is that?

* * *

The NEWS Talent Show was rubbish and the programme-makers don't seem to have made up their minds whether to disguise the contestants' horrendous lack of ability by using lots of strong backing singers, etc., or to go for broke with the sort of so-bad-it's-compelling car-crash TV.

*

The roads service has marked a pothole in our avenue with a big blue X. Our youngest child spotted it from his bedroom window and is now of the belief that there is buried treasure under the road outside our house.

*

I wonder if my prospective employers have read my application yet.

* * *

I've an interview! I've not had a job interview for approximately one hundred years! What do I wear? What do I talk about? It's next Monday.

* * *

Eleanor has lent me a skirt and top for the interview. I think it'll probably be obvious that I'm wearing someone else's clothes, but as my own consist mainly of tracksuit bottoms and T-shirts that have lost their vertical alignment in the wash, I don't have much option. She says they'll ask me if I'm willing to work Saturdays, and I must say yes, even though it means leaving him to look after the children. She says they'll also ask how I can be sure that I'll be able to cope with turning up for work every day when I've been at home for so long, and I'm to say that looking after small children means no lunch breaks, no holidays and no sick days, so that, by comparison, going out to work will be a doddle. She said to say that I've very supportive parents who will be happy to provide childcare as and when required. (I was afraid to ask her whether she actually meant this, as it would be a new development, or whether it was just something she was advising me to put forward for the purposes of getting the job.)

Eleanor also told me that they always ask what you would do if you found a puddle on the floor, and that this is a sort of trick question designed to catch out the two kinds of people who would either wipe it up themselves or leave it for someone else. Eleanor says you have to say you would wipe it up to remove the immediate hazard, but you must also say you would tell management in case the puddle is coming from a leak, or in case they want to surround the area with those yellow plastic men for insurance purposes until they're satisfied that everything is one hundred per cent dry and slip-free.

* * *

The *Mac* video came in the post today, along with a signed photograph of Harry Ferris in a tuxedo. He is the DJ who put out the call for me. I already knew what Harry Ferris looked like. As with most of the Zero FM crowd, he's been doing the same job for years and years and they all turn up on local TV from time to time, such as for the New Year's Eve party, etc. I must say, Harry's photo more than does him justice. If the camera is to be believed, he has considerably more hair now than when he was knocking back the vodkas on telly at Hogmanay.

The recording is on DVD, not VHS, which means I can't have a sneaky watch of it while the children are in school because I need them to put it on.

* * *

Some people are natural horn-tooters and others are not. The first lot can somehow find a variety of tones in their car-horn, depending on whether they want to say, 'Hello, old friend, how are you?', or 'Watch out, bicycle, just letting you know I'm here and about to come past' or 'Don't even think about trying to pull out in front of me' or even 'Fuck you, too.' Their horn-tooting is articulate. Then there is the second lot, who can only make their car-horn say: 'Bwehhh!' All we ever do – for of course I belong to the latter category – is startle people.

Today, as I was driving home, I saw Kathleen, Lorna and the double buggy going along the footpath ahead of me and tried for a friendly little toot that would say, 'Hello, Happy Grannies and your charges!' But it came out as 'Bwehhh!' which made Kathleen and Lorna nearly topple off the pavement under my wheels. They didn't recognise me or the car, although possibly this was due to its just having been washed (again).

I had left the job interview with £5 in my purse – enough for coffee with chocolate cheesecake at Mumbles or another trip to the Suds Bros hot-foam car-wash. It was no contest. I was a little disappointed that there wasn't any queue, as this meant the experience didn't last as long – but, oh, what a thrill as they turned on the power-hoses and started to jet me down. I sort of forget it's actually the car they're washing. It's a bit like being massaged, but without the embarrassing contact.

Speaking of which, I'm in *his* bad books again, and it's sex-related, as usual. First, he got a bit huffy because I wanted to watch the taped belated episode of *Mac* in bed last night (it was – as always – brilliant). Then, when that was finished and we were trying to establish an atmosphere of intimacy, I accidentally referred to his nightshirt as a 'nurtshite', an error I found implausibly amusing. I couldn't stop myself laughing every time it came back into my head. He thought I was feigning jollity to avoid sexual contact and went into a major sulk. I admit, in the cold light of day, 'nurtshite' doesn't strike me as quite so humorous as it did at midnight last night, but I wasn't pretending to laugh so I now have to face the possibility that even my real laugh sounds fake.

*

There was no laughing at the interview, real or otherwise. The worst part was sitting in the waiting area where my

24

hands grew cold and clammy and my intestines felt like they were incubating diarrhoea. My only companion was Gillian, scheduled for the slot immediately before me. She was built like a wrestler and fresh back from travelling in the Antipodes. I bet she could fold a map as well as the next man. After she was summoned, I went over and over my spiel in my head, so that by the time I was facing the panel I was excessively eager with my answers. When they asked me the 'puddle' question – as Eleanor, always right, had promised they would – I was so ready with my response that little glances were exchanged. I don't know if those glances said, 'This is the most over-rehearsed answer we've ever had' or 'My goodness, this woman thinks of everything.' They were all smiles as they said goodbye, but this might have been because I was the last candidate of the day and they were looking forward to a biscuit and a cup of tea. They said they'd let me know by the end of the week.

I have to get this job. It's a nine to one. job share and doesn't require any knowledge of spreadsheets. How often does one of those come along?

*

Little Diana Thornton from Radio 3 won *The North, East, West, South Talent Show*, beating Dermot Murnaghan into second place. Nobody had heard of her at the start of the week so she was lucky the phone-in vote didn't leave her out in the cold in the early stages, but when they gave her 'Pie Jesu' to sing on Wednesday she brought the house down. She sang it again last night in the final, along with 'I Know Him So Well' and 'Fields of Gold'. Against that line-up, even Dermot's 'Mack the Knife' didn't stand a chance.

*

My Mac is back tonight. Joy.

* * *

This morning I asked what was to be the news for News Day, and it was: 'My mummy had a job interview.' Despite the potential embarrassment to myself, I hadn't the heart to try to talk him out of it. He's so keen on the prospective novelty of his mother having a real job. To tell the truth, so am I.

*

There was a twist in last night's episode of *Mac*. This week's culprit is the psychological profiler Mac sometimes uses to get insight into his cases, and, because he's a profiler, he knows exactly how to send Mac in the wrong direction. This is the last story of the series, and, as everyone suspects that Lorcan Hinds, who plays Mac, wants a crack at Hollywood, there's the distinct possibility that he's about to kill off his character. I'll be bereft.

* * *

Poor little Diana Thornton. Her fifteen minutes of fame has backfired already. In the supermarket this morning I saw that, although her picture was on most of the front pages with some chirpy gossip attached, a tabloid declared 'Secret

Shame of Wee Di.' Of course I stopped and read the intro. It seems that Diana has been outed by a girlhood friend as a late bed-wetter who had to wear incontinence pads at sleepovers. Does the fact that Andrew Lloyd Webber is rumoured to be offering her a leading-lady role in his next West End production outweigh this revelation?

*

We were left not knowing whether Mac died. That is to say, the profiler had Mac in a tight corner and Mac was trying to talk his way out of being assassinated, but it all depended on how charismatic Mac would turn out to be, which we had to judge for ourselves. I think Lorcan Hinds is hedging his bets in case Hollywood doesn't want him. How could they not?

* * *

A vellum envelope has come, with my name and address in a beautiful, artistic hand. I can't open it, such is its power to thwart my small but important dream of a paid job.

*

Oh, my God, I got the job!

*

I. Got. The. Job.

*

!

*

I really thought I'd blown it when I said in my interview that I'd turn a blind eye to the old woman stealing a tin of cat-food.

*

As of next Monday, I'm the new Job-share (Mornings) Undercover Store Detective at the Riverside shopping mall!

* * *

Moira Reynolds rang me this morning and asked me to pop in for an initial chat about the job. I was torn between being eager to get cracking and that I was still in my housework tracksuit bottoms and twisty T-shirt. Now that I'm a working woman I must observe a minimum level of presentability at all times. I asked her to give me an hour and I'd be there. Moira Reynolds is the human-resources manager at the Riverside shopping mall. She sat in the middle of the interview panel.

When I got to the mall I had to go to Customer Services and ask for Moira, who had said she would come down and meet me to give me the tour. I did my best to seem pleasant to the Customer Services girl because, after all, I'm going to be her colleague soon, but she'd a special knack of keeping her face impassive and her voice silent as she turned to the internal phone and dialled Moira's number. I wondered whether I'd only imagined I'd spoken, and then if I was still at home in bed, dreaming this encounter, but then she spoke into the mouthpiece and I gathered she was telling Moira of my arrival.

I could have sat on one of the nearby benches to wait, but I thought that might seem lazy and I wanted to create a good impression so I looked about for something that would make me appear a bit brighter and more industrious. The best I could come up with was to browse the newspaper stand, which was still full of little Diana Thornton – the tabloids talking about her, and the broadsheets analysing all the fuss the tabloids were making. There was nothing about Dermot Murnaghan – nobody remembers who came second. And then Moira was there.

Moira walks very quickly, even in high heels, I discovered, as I tried to keep up. She talks quickly, too. In less than half an hour she'd swept me round every business in the mall and introduced me to as many of the shop staff as possible – quietly in front of customers as it would have been madness to blow my cover. And that was the main problem, she said, and the reason why my contract was only for five months. The customers start to recognise you for what you are so you are no longer undercover. (I'm not a high-profile security guard with a deterrent function – they've big burly guys in epaulettes for that. I am meant to be the unnoticed one who creeps about witnessing acts of shoplifting and has the culprit brought before management, then the police.)

I did know the job was only for five months, but I'd assumed this was to provide the real store detective with maternity cover. It turns out that the previous incumbent – a man – has already left, which is why they want me to start so quickly. My job-share partner isn't even Gillian but a woman I didn't meet at the interview, Michelle, who is doing a university access course in the mornings. Moira said they always get loads of applications for store detectives from body-builders like Gillian, and also from ex-service personnel and retired police officers, but they've stopped using them because such people are too visible and thieves can spot them a mile off. Apparently people like Michelle and me are much better at slipping about unnoticed.

When we had done all the shops, Moira whisked me upstairs in the staff-and-goods lift to show me the employees' cloakroom, where she produced a locker key. (I'm far too excited about getting my own locker!) Standing beside me in front of the mirror she told me that the way I had dressed was fine for work because dressing up would make me stand out from the crowd. (Little did she know that, for me, this was dressed up. I was wearing my 'smart' jeans.)

Finally, she took me to the staff canteen and got me an instant sachet cappuccino for nothing, although I'll be expected to pay in future, and I must keep my purse in my locker: employees are not allowed to carry money anywhere on the shop floor. The canteen is subsidised, though. Instant sachet cappuccinos are only 30p and I'll be able to get a hot meal for £1.50 at the end of my shift before I set off for school.

While I wouldn't like to say Moira hadn't done a

thorough job of introducing me to the mall, it was all kind of general stuff, which would have been the same if I'd been starting as a checkout girl. Really, I felt I needed to know more about how an undercover store detective operates, so I was glad when she asked if I'd any questions.

I learned that I'm basically to spend my time walking about the shops, always wearing my coat and carrying an empty handbag, and probably at least one plastic bag from some shop in the mall, filled with goods I've to sign for and return. I'm to pretend to browse, but without buying or removing any items, and I'm to look out for thieves. In the event that I spot an act of shoplifting, I'm to engage the help of a member of that shop's staff, and if the culprit leaves without paying, we're to follow and challenge them. But I must be one hundred per cent sure that the person has stolen something: shoplifting is a massive problem at the Riverside mall, but being sued for wrongful apprehension could potentially be even worse. I asked Moira how many shop-lifters a day it was normal to confront. Moira said she didn't want to over-excite me, but usually none. However, she was sure I was the breath of fresh air who would change that. Just so long as I understood the importance of never chal-lenging an innocent person.

Am I nervous? I am, yes. I am.

*

I couldn't help noticing, as we went round, that the Riverside shopping mall has a very high ratio of cafés, etc., to shops.

How can they all survive? There's the juice bar (whose days are definitely numbered: people round here are suspicious of any café where the leading beverage isn't 'a cup of tea'), there's the supermarket café where Shouting Barbara and the man with two hats read the free newspapers, there's Sandwich, Sandwich, the filled-baguetterie, which has moved down from the high street, there's the gourmet coffee place, which is lovely even to walk past for its aroma – but the prices, like the cups, are colossal – and, of course, there's the Tasty Ranch just outside the front door. In terms of shops there's the supermarket, the discount designer shop, the sports shop, Diggers Discount Jewellery, the stationery shop with pretensions to be a bookshop because it keeps a few racks of new releases and best-sellers, Pharmacity the chemist chain, Shoerama, Nursery World and that very badly lit shop for young women's cheap fashions.

The mall's walkway is finished off with some nice wooden bench seating, some fake plant displays with gravel round them to keep down the imaginary weeds, and the inevitable grabber machines. Some of the women in the canteen were complaining about them. Seemingly, customers are constantly losing money in them, but nobody in the building is authorised to give a refund because the man who owns them and others like them in shopping centres across the land doesn't live anywhere near our town, and punters are supposed to write to him if they experience difficulty. I noticed that Moira avoided getting involved in this conversation. She struck me as someone who is fiercely loyal to her employers and would never be heard criticising them. When I asked her if it was true that Argos is coming to the bit of waste ground behind the mall she was very tight-lipped indeed.

* * *

I'm a heroine! I'm the talk of the Riverside shopping mall! I've executed my first 'bust' on my very first day, and it was a really big one!

It started this morning when I was walking across from the supermarket to the wannabe bookshop. I can't stroll – that makes it too obvious that I'm not purposefully shopping – so I only caught a passing glimpse, but I was pretty sure I saw two women unloading a pram from the hatch of a nearby small car. Nothing strange there, except that by the time they were entering the mall, they appeared not to know each other.

Well, as it happened, I'd seen this before. Once, when I was working in the Listening Angels thrift shop, we had two women come into the shop like that and while one, who was pretending to be pregnant, feigned a dizzy fit and distracted us, her accomplice loaded up with goods. We caught them, through the vigilance of Shouting Barbara, a naïve-but-not stupid 'character' about town, who was hidden behind the changing-room curtain. I could see that something similar might be afoot here. I had to watch and wait, but it didn't take long.

Soon the woman with the pram went into Nursery World, followed a few seconds later by her estranged companion. I ventured forward. Holding up one little velour outfit after another to give myself an excuse to look in Mrs Pram's direction, as Mrs No Pram had gone to ask something at the counter, I rapidly formed the impression that there was no baby in that conveyance. The counter assistant was now leading Mrs No Pram to the back of the shop and climbing onto a kick-step with her back turned to stretch for something a little out of reach. A second assistant appeared from behind a nearby 'Staff Only' door and the first assistant stopped her, too, and she got involved in the exchange.

But what was Mrs Pram doing? She was very quickly swapping the well-worn model with which she'd entered the shop for a brand-new one from the display, slinging her handbag over the handle and leaving Nursery World with no intention of paying!

I charged over to the assistants, hissed, 'Shoplifter! She took your pram!' and belted out into the walkway. Right behind me followed the accomplice, who wasn't going to hang about, closely pursued by the assistant who hadn't been perched on the kick-step.

Two lucky things happened. First, Mrs Stolen Pram decided to abandon the vehicle and make a run for it, except her handbag strap had slid down and got stuck between the handle and the carriage and she got caught up trying to free it. Second, Tony the epauletted security guy was standing right where we needed him, by the front doors, and wasn't going to let any sprinting figures, with us scurrying after them like Cagney and Lacey, leave the building.

As it turned out, when Moira came downstairs with Ted Twome, the mall's deputy manager, the stolen pram was filled with stolen baby clothes and blankets. The women had loaded it on Sunday evening when the staff were too tired to notice, put the covers on and left it ready for collection on Monday morning.

The Nursery World assistants thought I was great and seemed generally quite excited that such a heist had been attempted on their premises. Ted Twome congratulated me on hitting the jackpot on my first day. Moira was a little more measured. I don't think she wants me to get too big ideas about myself just yet. But I was quietly pleased with my adventure. Through the entire episode, right until the shouting and running had started, nobody had noticed me watching. I'd always thought I was invisible in this town. Now my invisibility had a use.

* * *

It was with a mixture of pride and guilt that I told last night's meeting of the Parents' Committee that I'm unable to do playground-parent duty any more, due to gainful employment. While there were congratulations on my getting a job – even a temporary one – I could feel people thinking what a waste of money it had been having my police check done, and it was this knowledge, plus the fact that I wanted to get home in time to watch the new Bill Worthington mystery, which made me offer to write the questions for the Spring Quiz. When I got home, *he* said I'm mad and have no idea how much work will be involved, but I'm pleased: if I'm in charge of the questions, there's no way I'll also be asked to take responsibility for the dreaded tea-boilers – my biggest worry about being involved with the Parents' Committee.

*

(I couldn't tell the committee about the Great Pram Robbery because I'm not allowed to talk to anyone outside work about incidents of collaring criminals in case such gossip could affect a prosecution. But I had earlier vented my euphoria, secretly and alone, by treating myself to another hot-foam car-wash. I didn't use Suds Bros but instead went to the Wash 'n' Go. I told myself it was just for a change, but I suspect the true reason was that I don't want the staff at Suds Bros to think I've got a bit of a kink about car-washes.)

*

Bill Worthington's daughter, Jenny, was taken hostage last night, so his wry smile was put on hold for the evening and replaced by his grim look, which he sustained for the duration. I think Jenny Worthington's a bit of a little madam and too old to assume, as she invariably does, that every time her parents are invited somewhere she is too. She's an only child and, I think, spoilt rotten. Although she must have passed thirty, she's clearly not going to leave home properly until Bill and Grace hand over a huge deposit to get her on the property ladder. So, last night's 'drama' was a bit of a flop for me as I couldn't have cared less whether Jenny Worthington was found in time or not. (She was, of course. Isn't it amazing how it takes Bill and his sergeant exactly one hour and fifty-five minutes to solve every mystery? Just for one week, wouldn't it be fun if they solved it in the first twenty minutes so we'd get a look at what they did afterwards?) Anyhow, although it was Bill himself who finally unlocked the puzzle, he had to radio ahead to young Sergeant Samson, who was conveniently nearer than he to the barn where Jenny was tied to a chair, so we could go from distraught parent to love interest in one move. Telly's so predictable, isn't it? I don't know why I watch so much of it.

*

It occurs to me that the optimum time to rob the Riverside shopping mall is eleven o'clock, as this is when I'm ordered to take my break. The burly epaulettes, Tony and Leon, go earlier, separately, so that there are always two of us on the shop floor at any given time. But as I'm the only one whose job it is to detect, rather than deter shoplifters, I'm the one you've really got to watch, which is difficult because I'm undercover.

At home, everyone's making fun of my job. They act as though I'm a cross between a secret agent and Harry Potter. But, to be serious, the Riverside loses a hell of a lot of money via shoplifting, so my job isn't all that funny. Sometimes *he* seems to think properly about it and tells me not to take any stupid risks, as it's only a job, and then I'd rather he went back to joking again because it makes me afraid that somebody I apprehend may turn on me, punch me in the face or produce a knife. I don't want to think about that.

*

An odd thing happened today in the canteen. As I was waiting at the serving hatch for my cup of tea (15p!) to go with my tuna and mayonnaise roll (35p!), an expensively dressed, vaguely familiar woman came in and threw herself, with her large, glamorous bag, down at a table with some shop girls. When I'd left the hatch and sat down with my roll, she went up and got herself an instant sachet cappuccino and a salad, and I did that thing I sometimes do of looking at someone for far too long, to the point at which she turned round and sent a dagger straight in my direction. I blushed so hard into my lunch that I could scarcely swallow anything, which didn't help me to make the hasty escape I wished for. But I cannot stop wondering who she was. I'm sure I know her from somewhere. She was wearing a pair of sunglasses on top of her striking silver-fox spiky hair. (It's January.)

* * *

I've decided to write five quiz questions every day. These are today's:

1. By what other name is the plant woodbine better known?

2. 'Dixie' or 'Dixieland' is the popular name for the southern states of the USA, south of which line?
3. Which confectionery manufacturer makes Aero chocolate?
4. Who described a cynic as 'A man who knows the price of everything and the value of nothing?'
5. In the TV series *Porridge*, what were the first two names of central character Fletcher?

Answers:
1. Honeysuckle.
2. The Mason–Dixon line.
3. Nestlé.
4. Oscar Wilde (in *Lady Windermere's Fan*).
5. Norman Stanley.

*

Michelle-the-university-access-course-woman, who takes over from me at the Riverside in the afternoons, has a funny little gesture that annoys me. As I go off duty and she comes on, which takes place in a dark corner by the staff-and-goods lift, she always gives me a very serious high-five, as if I were an off-coming footballer and she my substitute. Frankly, I find this embarrassing, and a little weird, but I haven't the heart to walk past her and leave her hand floating in the air.

*

He says I've made the quiz questions too hard. By which he means, I suspect, that he cannot answer them.

* * *

When I got to the canteen at lunchtime, the good-looking silver-fox woman was already there, flicking through one of the complimentary papers that come up from the supermarket news-stand. I tried strenuously not to look at her while I ate my cheese and tomato baton (40p), but when Moira Reynolds came in, the woman greeted her and I stole the chance to look across. As Moira sat down with her, I think she called the woman 'Lyn.' Lyn, Lyn, Lyn . . . this rings a bell. I'm sure I should know who she is. But why would I know a woman who works in the Riverside shopping mall? And does she work in it? She doesn't look like a shop-worker. Is she management? Or does she perhaps own it?

*

Sometimes, as I approach the canteen, I get a vague smell, like bad eggs. This makes me slightly selective about what I choose to eat. Not the egg mayonnaise, for example.

*

1. I'm an American-born British novelist and critic. I settled in England in 1876, and in my early novels dealt with the relationship between European civilisation and American life, notably in *The Portrait of a Lady* (1881). In *The Bostonians* (1886), I portrayed American society in its own right, then produced many novels of English life. I'm also remembered for my ghost story, *The Turn of the Screw* (1898). Who am I? .

2. Which element has the chemical symbol Ag?
3. Of which Shakespeare hero does Horatio say: 'Now cracks a noble heart. Good night, sweet prince: / And flights of Angels sing thee to thy rest!'? [I have always thought Hamlet was a bit of a pain in the arse, not only with all that dithering but also with those endless bloody puns. Laertes was a lot more dynamic, at least as noble and much less irritating with his use of language – so why does nobody say so?]
4. Which beverage comes in the varieties English Breakfast, Afternoon Blend and Earl Grey?
5. Who is the long-serving presenter of the weekday breakfast show, from seven thirty to nine thirty, on Radio 2?

Answers:
1. Henry James.
2. Silver.
3. Hamlet.
4. Tea.
5. Terry Wogan.

*

It might not have been 'Lyn'. It might have been 'Linda'. Who, who, who is that woman? I feel I should know.

*

The symptoms of the hot-foam car-wash fixation are spreading, like a rash: now I am stimulated by hot soapy water in general. Not only do I stand mesmerised watching the bath run but I even rush towards the sensual pleasure of washing the children's lunchboxes in the afternoon – a chore I used to put off until bedtime because I found it so irksome.

*

Today I caught two girls from the posh school stealing cosmetics from the supermarket. I might not have had the steel to go through with it if I'd thought they'd be prosecuted, but the Riverside has a policy of not pressing charges with first-offence schoolchildren. They're happy enough to send them home to their parents in a marked police car, which tends to do the trick. Of course, I might have been wrong about them being first offenders, but I knew I wasn't. I'd a hunch – like Mac – that seasoned professionals wouldn't do all that noisy giggling, hair-flicking and performing for one another.

At their age, I wouldn't have noticed me watching, either. I followed them out and nodded to Tony, who helped me stop and challenge them.

Ted Twome and Moira came down again, then they and Tony took the girls upstairs in the staff-and-goods lift to wait for the police. I went straight back to work, but it's hard to settle when you've just done what I had. It's not exciting, exactly, but adrenalin's involved. I prowled about a bit faster than usual, not taking much in. So, maybe that's the optimum time to rob premises: just after somebody else has been caught and everyone's in a bit of a lather.

42

*

He didn't get the question on Henry James but feels this round is better than the first.

* * *

The mystery of the silver-fox woman has been solved by none other than Kathleen and Lorna. I bumped into my friends as they came into the Riverside today with their surrogate grandchildren to buy Nathan's night-time nappy-pants on special offer in Pharmacity. (I'm encouraged to stop and talk to my real-life friends and acquaintances as this helps authenticate my disguise as a member of the public.) Well, they were full of it. They'd just been hailed and spoken to by a certain silver-haired Lindy-May Coulthard, who had admired the boys and asked Kathleen and Lorna if they were the children's grannies – to which they'd felt obliged to reply with a brief explanation of the Happy Grannies scheme. (Did they think they'd go to hell if they just said, 'Yes'?) But Lindy-May Coulthard! Of course! Of *The Lindy-May Morning Show* on Zero FM. She's been broadcasting there for as long as I can remember. She's in the slot right after Harry Ferris.

But what is she doing in our staff canteen?

Before she'd hurried on, Lindy-May had asked Kathleen and Lorna if the boys were twins. Shows how much she knows about children. They might share a double buggy, but Nathan is twice the age and size of Samuel.

Lindy-May has a daily quiz on her show. Marilyn and I

used to do it on Friday mornings at the market. (Marilyn wasn't very good. I was sometimes amazed at the stuff she didn't know, for a former special-needs teacher.) Perhaps I could ask Lindy-May for some tips on setting a quiz that will please all of the people all of the time.

She lives somewhere near here, now that I think about it. I seem to remember she moved out of the city and bought some old place with stables so that she could ride her horse every day.

But what is she doing in our staff canteen?

*

Today I caught my first man. (In a manner of speaking.) At the supermarket checkout I saw him pay for the litre of milk, *Daily Mirror* and steak-and-kidney-pie-in-a-tin that he had in his basket, but fail to disclose the flat half-bottle of cheap Scotch whisky he'd slid up his overcoat sleeve. This now establishes conclusively that I'm indistinguishable to the naked eye of women, minors and, predictably, men.

*

Lindy-May has a beautifully shaped head. (It's my theory that human beings pair off according to a hierarchy of head shapes, rather than any other attribute.) You can see that, if the worst happened and she were to lose her stunning silver-fox hair, even bald she would look good. My head would look like a thin, pointy egg.

*

As I was having lunch today (tuna and pasta bake and a glass of cranberry juice, 75p – I still can't get over it), sitting with one of the supermarket girls and one from Nursery World, Moira Reynolds came over and asked me for a word. I thought I was in trouble, possibly for staring at a certain minor celebrity of our airwaves, but no. Moira just wanted to say that I seem to have settled in really well, and management were pleased with my results, which were impressive and even unexpected for a first week. (The Nursery World girl had just told me that Michelle, my high-fiving colleague, hasn't nabbed a single robber.)

I thought, Isn't that just the way? When I finally find my forte, I'm only allowed to do it for five short months. But never mind, at least they like me. And that's another thing Moira said: it's good that I stay around to have my lunch and chat with other staff after my shift instead of rushing off. She thinks it helps me and the others to feel I'm part of the team, especially as I've to behave as though I'm on my lonely ownsome when I'm on the shop floor.

Rush off without having my lunch? Moira grossly underestimates the draw of a subsidised canteen.

I don't have to work Saturdays and Sundays. They have two university students to do that.

*

Today, from the back bedroom window, I saw Lucy out weeding. I'm glad she's feeling better. I think she believes in Candide's wise motto: 'Cultivate your garden.' We have let our dwarf rhododendrons sicken terribly, and only the dandelions truly thrive. I'd love to tell her I've got over the anxiety that benighted my structureless months after the fall of the Angels, and that I even have a new job, but Tom is never far away. He clearly believes that merely talking to me will make Lucy's brain bleed spontaneously.

But things aren't so bad. I've my job, my crime dramas and my own little mystery to solve: what is Lindy-May doing in our staff canteen?

* * *

In celebration and expectation of my first monthly pay-packet – or, rather, my first electronic credit to our building-society current account, which isn't as romantic – we took the children to the seaside for the weekend. I like the seaside in winter. I like the bracing walks on the beach, the sleepy cafés and the arcades where the savvy local children hang around, like old men in a betting shop. We got on quite well, probably because it was a day for saying 'yes' to most things that people wanted to do. The adults let their hair down and went on the swings and the slide in the empty play-park. And, of course, a little cash eases most situations, doesn't it?

Fish and chips always taste best at the seaside.

*

After being away from my new job for two whole days, I got nervous all over again about going back. Mine is a strange, nomadic role, and it isn't very affirming that my colleagues have to blank me. I might easily feel unloved. The canteen is my little haven: people are nearly always friendly to me there, possibly because most of us are nosy and quite enjoy hearing about trouble. I, of course, am the agent of trouble and also 'the horse's mouth'.

Today at my break (toast with Marmite and tea, 25p) I sat with Cheryl, who looks like a model and does public relations and marketing for the Riverside. She wasn't after tales of petty crime and punishment, though, as she's up to her eyes organising a bonny-baby competition in conjunction with the local paper. Next week a mobile photographer will set up his lights, parasol and backdrop in front of the grabber machines and take competition-entry portraits for £9.99. (Full sets of prints will also, of course, be available.) The paper will print the pictures, along with a voting form. Ted Twome has really got behind the project, according to Cheryl, and helped her put up posters all over town.

When Cheryl had drunk her hot-water-with-a-slice-of-lemon, eaten her Weightwatchers yogurt and left, I asked Brenda, the cigarette-counter assistant, if Ted Twome is married. He is. If Ted and Cheryl are not already having an affair, then they're about to. Trust me, I've a nose for these things.

*

Tonight's drama is one of those vile, grisly ones where they delight in showing you death in close-up and Technicolor. That's not why I watch television!

* * *

What a day! The staff-and-goods lift got stuck. With me in it. Had I been on my own, I might have panicked about being in a confined space with limited oxygen, but luckily I wasn't. I was with the most confident woman in town: Lindy-May.

Three things about Lindy-May. She never stops moving, she never stops talking, and she has very little sense of discretion. While we were stuck in that lift, waiting for the engineer, she took off her high heels, put on her high heels, sprayed herself with perfume, reapplied her lipstick, reapplied her mascara, tried and failed to get a signal on her mobile, took a swig from a little bottle she kept in her bag, pumped up her spiky silver-fox hair, flicked through *Hello!* magazine, blew her nose and did one side of a Rubik's cube, which she apparently carries for such emergencies. I wouldn't have been surprised if she'd whipped out a yo-yo.

The stream of activity was accompanied by a stream of chatter, which only required the minimum encouragement from me, and was entertaining, really. She talked about the goings-on at the radio station, and which of the presenters is doing a line with which of the researchers, and who hates their producer, and how she has a bit of an on-and-off thing with Harry Ferris, who, she says, is getting a weave soon. And then she talked about her horse, Rasputin, and why he's better than any man, though she wouldn't kick Lorcan

Hinds out of bed. (She has actually interviewed Lorcan Hinds and said he is even more mesmerising in the flesh than on the telly and is simply the best-smelling man she's ever encountered.)

I also discovered that Lindy-May hadn't looked daggers at me that day. As far as she was concerned, today was the first time she'd set eyes on me (invisible, invisible). She said if I ever think I see her looking cross it means she's taken out her contacts, unless she's genuinely cross and then I'll know all about it. The reason she uses our staff canteen as her own personal café is because she gets pestered in public. People stare at her or come up and ask for autographs or even openly discuss her where she can hear them. When she comes off air, she wants to pop in somewhere she can be one of the gang and have her cappuccino in peace.

I was fated to spend this afternoon with Lindy-May – right down to the fact that Eleanor was collecting the children from school so I didn't have to worry about them. And also right down to the fact that Lindy-May was looking for someone unlike herself – quiet, discreet, still, unremarkable – to do a special job for her (for payment). I'm sure she's mixing up store detective (i.e., amateur) with actual detective (i.e., professional), but I said 'yes' when she asked me. Because she'd stopped being so confident and seemed almost vulnerable. Lindy-May of *The Lindy-May Morning Show* wants me to find her missing brother.

* * *

1. What is the name of the coffee shop frequented by the characters in *Friends*?
2. Which character from Greek mythology was almost invincible except for a vulnerable spot at his heel?
3. Whose 2005 debut album was entitled *Back to Bedlam*?

Answers:

1. Central Perk.
2. Achilles.
3. James Blunt.

I'm writing questions because I don't want to think about what I've done. *He* says I've really lost it now and have begun to delude myself that I actually am a detective. Which is hard to refute because I have taken on a commission to locate a missing person. He's right. I've gone mad. I have to tell Lindy-May I can't do it. I suspect she won't be an easy woman to say 'no' to. When did I imagine I'd do it? I now work every weekday morning and I have the children in the afternoons. Oh, if only I hadn't got into that lift yesterday. In future, I'm taking the stairs.

* * *

This morning, as I was prowling around Pharmacity, a girl from the posh school was trying out samples at the cosmetics stand. I was pretending to look at toothpastes, when I saw her brazenly stick a lip-gloss into her blazer pocket. As I continued watching, she went on to take a mascara, then something else I couldn't see. She doused herself in scent at the perfumery counter and left the shop with that self-assured lilting glide that all the posh girls seem to adopt.

I looked to the counter assistant for support, but she was occupied with one customer while two more were forming a queue, and her colleague must have been on her break. I followed the posh girl out into the walkway where, luckily, I thought, I saw Leon the burly security guy, not far off. But when I tried to get his attention, he was distracted by something in the other direction and turned away. I looked about in desperation for anyone who could accompany me to challenge the girl, but there was no one. Eventually I had to let her go.

It was the first time I'd witnessed an offence but been forced to let the culprit escape. It unsettled me.

*

Lindy-May hasn't been in the canteen for the past couple of days. Perhaps she can't face me. Perhaps she wishes she'd never told me about her missing brother and hopes I'll forget about the whole thing.

*

I've started washing bits of the house with hot soapy water just for the thrill of it. Last night I did the kitchen floor, and tonight the cupboard fronts. I don't know if it's down to my new attraction to steamy water or whether it's because I'm now out of the house in the mornings, but I'm discovering a sort of thirst for physical, gritty domestic toil. And I crave products. Ever since I read that newspaper article about toxic chemicals in the home I've been doing everything with bicarbonate of soda and a bottle of Ecover. I'm sick of them. I yearn for the smells of bleach and Mr Sheen.

*

I've looked in the *Yellow Pages* and there are such things as private detectives. I'll tell Lindy-May.

* * *

I'd convinced myself that if I got through to the weekend without any sign of Lindy-May, the finding-her-brother thing would go away. So my heart sank when I glanced up from my tuna-and-red-onion sandwich at lunchtime to see the back of her silver-fox head at the serving hatch. I knew she'd come to sit with me, and she did.

At first, I tried to engage her in small talk, of which I usually have none, but there was one matter on which I genuinely wanted to pick her brains. Her quiz. I thought she might be able to point me in the right direction, questions-wise. Unfortunately, it turned out that although Lindy-May asks the questions, she doesn't write them. Hilary, her producer, does that. Then I thought I'd try to get away but Lindy-May grabbed my hand and held on to it.

I tried to be rational, but I was leaning forward in my seat with my ankles crossed under the chair. I couldn't untangle them and get them flat on the floor to 'ground' myself, as we had been taught during my brief encounter with T'ai Chi last year, so it was hopeless.

I struggled to explain that I didn't know how to look for a missing person, and that I'd three children to manage when I wasn't at the Riverside, but Lindy-May looked desolate and asked if I couldn't take the children out searching with me. I tried to tell her about the private detectives in the *Yellow Pages* but she already knew. She said she couldn't use them in case they went to the local scandal rag and then her brother would never forgive her.

She gave me two pages torn out of a shorthand notebook. They said her brother was called Mark Strain (Coulthard was Lindy-May's first husband's name: her original name was Linda Margaret Strain, but she didn't think it was commercial) and he was forty-one. The last person to have seen him was his girlfriend, Tanya, with whom he had lived in one of the new canal-side apartments in the town until she had kicked him out a week before Christmas. He had phoned Lindy-May on Christmas Eve, but she'd been unable to find out where he was or what his plans were and hadn't been able to get hold of him since. It was six weeks since anyone had set eyes on him.

I folded up the pieces of paper. I really didn't want to get involved. Summoning all my courage, I asked Lindy-May if she couldn't look for her brother herself. I pointed out that as she knew so many little things about him she'd be the person best qualified for the job. But Lindy-May replied that, despite what I might think, Zero FM made you a household name round here, and it would be all over the country like wildfire if it were known she was trying to track down a missing family member, whereas . . . (Whereas no one would notice me, was what she would have said. She was probably right.) She gave me a snapshot of her brother, taken at a party. He's handsome and hasn't yet gone grey, unlike his sister.

*

The slight rotten-egg smell was present in the corridor by the canteen again.

*

I took the car through the car-wash to scrub away the grime of a wearing day. When they whited out the windows with foam the children shrieked with delight and pretended they were in a blizzard. I wished we could stay there for a long time.

My energy was so sapped by today's happenings that I could only be bothered to make potato waffles for tea. If I take on this extra work in the afternoons, there'll be a lot more of that kind of thing.

* * *

I'm acting out of character. This afternoon when I parked outside Tanya's flat, I left the two older children in the car and took the youngest one in with me. I bought them all Sherbet Dabs to keep them occupied while I did my work. (I never buy the children sweets, because I don't want them to end up with teeth like mine.)

Having absolutely no idea how to conduct myself like a detective, I did what I've seen on television. I took a good look round in case anyone was watching me approach Tanya's flat. Then, having discerned no one, I rang the bell. I'd no ID to flash when she opened the door, other than my AA membership card or my library ticket, so I settled for telling her my name and introducing my child, whom I prompted to greet this stranger in a friendly fashion. Tanya, who has a light-beige hall rug, blocked our way until we had wiped our feet satisfactorily.

Tanya is like a cameo in *The Bill*. You can imagine her described in the script as 'Missing Bloke's Girlfriend: gold jewellery, big earrings, big hair, long legs.' (I found myself wondering where on earth she buys her tights. Surely normal ones would only come up to her knees.)

She showed us into the main room. It had french windows, noisy laminate flooring, cream sofas – I saw her look with distaste at the sherbet dab – and a black-leather recliner chair. There was 'fashion' artwork on the walls – the kind you buy from interiors stores to match your decor, rather than as stand-alone pieces from galleries – and a fake fireplace set with a tied bunch of dry sticks. I could smell vanilla air-freshener.

Tanya took the lead, asking something like, 'So, what do you want to know?'

I wasn't quite ready for her. Wasn't it usual first to ask for a recent photograph of the missing person? But I already had the one Lindy-May had given me. I fished in my handbag and pulled it out, playing for time. I ad-libbed something like, 'Would you say this picture is a good likeness of Mark?'

Tanya took the picture. With me sitting and her standing, she towered over me. She handed it back, saying something like, 'I'd say that's a very good likeness. Yes.'

Looking more closely at the french windows, I saw they opened on to a railed balcony, which overhung the canal. In the context of a missing-person inquiry this seemed more ominous than it might have in, say, estate-agent-viewing circumstances.

I tried to remember again what they did on telly. They didn't panic, that was for sure, they just asked normal questions. I pretended I was Mac's sergeant, Charlotte Burnside, and asked Tanya to tell me about the last time she'd seen Mark.

*

Tonight I experienced a hot flush in the kitchen while I was doing the accounts and waiting for the potatoes to boil. Am I going to have an early menopause?

*

This morning, Caroline asked me at school how I'm getting on with the questions for the quiz. I said, 'Oh, fine, fine.' But

I'm not. I've contemplated stealing them from other sources, but *The Weakest Link*'s are too easy and *University Challenge*'s too hard. I've found a list of pet names for the American states in the back of our reference dictionary, but I can't realistically use more than one. Ditto *The Guinness Book of Hit Singles*.

* * *

Today, the photographer for the bonny-baby competition set up his stall in the mall. It didn't take him long. You can either get a straightforward colour picture of your child lying on a sheep's fleece, in which case he rolls down the blue-haze backdrop, or you can put them bare-armed and barefoot into a pair of denim dungarees from his rack of various sizes and he does a sepia shot of them on a bale of hay. You would be amazed how many are going for the hay. You wouldn't be amazed that the level of shrill noise has soared in the Riverside shopping mall: small children do not enjoy having their clothes changed for no good reason.

Cheryl and Ted Twome stood by for much of the morning, just watching, chatting and, presumably, congratulating themselves on how well the promotion seemed to be going. I stand by my theory about them.

*

There was no crime drama on telly last night. Instead we got an interactive documentary on the effects of global warming. To 'sex up' this subject, it was presented as a race between the polar ice caps melting and the rainforest burning down, and we, the viewers, had to phone in to say which we would save, if we could save only one. Mariella Frostrup put the case for the polar ice caps and John Craven for the rainforest.

*

I've looked at the names and addresses Tanya gave me for friends of Mark Strain. I must say, she doesn't seem much bothered by his disappearance but, then, she isn't his big sister. Lindy-May and Mark were orphaned when they were in their twenties, and I think this made them close. (Although not, unfortunately, close enough for Mark to tell Lindy-May where he has been for the past month.) I've informed Lindy-May that I'm going to start looking at the nearest friend's house. I stake it out this afternoon.

*

He has bought our youngest child *Lassie* on DVD because of the child's enthusiasm for dogs and our refusal to buy him one. Our youngest only sits still long enough to watch a film if it's pure slapstick, so unless Lassie's going to get hit on the head by a man swinging round with a plank, he can forget it.

*

Having neglected the manufacturer's instructions to dry it after each use, I see that our bathmat has formed black mould on its underside. Yuk. I lifted it between my finger and thumb and put it into the outside bin.

* * *

This morning, Ted Twome seconded me and Tony to crowd-control duties on the photographer's stand. Yesterday afternoon there had been squabbling among the mothers, and things had turned ugly. Tony used his bulk to keep the line in order, and I handed out dungarees to keep things moving as quickly as possible.

It was the first time I'd spent any time with Tony: I can't consort with him on the shop floor, and we're obliged to take our breaks at different times. I learned that he'd like to leave the mall and get a job as a personal trainer. After a while, Moira Reynolds came by. When she saw what I was doing, her face turned thunderous.

Five minutes later, Cheryl appeared and said I was to go on my break, then return to normal duties. In the canteen, Brenda told me Moira had got stuck into Ted like a day's work for displaying me as a member of staff before a line-up of every shoplifting mother in town!

*

When I'd picked up the children from school yesterday, I drove to the home of Mark's geographically closest friend and parked across the street. A lot of the houses have been converted to dentists' surgeries and architects' practices and things like that, so one more car wasn't particularly noticeable. I put on the tape of *The Owl Who Was Afraid of the Dark* for the children and prepared to wait.

After about half an hour, a man wearing a car coat over

a suit came out of the house and locked the door. I jumped out and ran across the road to him. I blurted something like, 'Excuse me, I'm looking for Mark Strain. Is he staying with you by any chance?'

He seemed bewildered and scanned the street as if something might pop up to explain my ambush. Then he said words to the effect that 'I'm just the surveyor. It's the owner of the house you're after.' I must have wilted visibly, because he told me then, in a kinder voice, that he thought the owner did have someone staying at the moment.

This was my first lead, but I had to go home to get the tea on.

*

We didn't go out anywhere this evening for Valentine's, but he gave me flowers – a proper bouquet, not just a bunch from the garage – and I bought him the new Van Morrison album. We said we'd rather wait and go out at the weekend when we wouldn't have to get up for work the next day.

*

I must look in Pharmacity tomorrow for a new bathmat.

* * *

Kathleen and Lorna brought Nathan and Samuel to have their photographs taken for the bonny-baby competition. They couldn't decide whether to go for the normal shot or the sepia cowboy effect, so they went back out to the Tasty Ranch for a snack and to think it over. Then Nathan got milkshake on his jumper, which made the decision for them. They joined the queue for dungarees. Somehow, I don't think the hillbilly look will appeal to Fiona and Simon.

*

The posh schoolgirl thief was back. Something isn't right there. I recognised her as soon as she bobbed elegantly through the doors. She said hello to Leon, who smiled and said hello, too. I recalled how he'd turned away the day she'd stolen the cosmetics when I'd needed him to nab her, and it crossed my mind that maybe something wasn't as it seemed. I kept my distance but followed her.

First she went into Shoerama. Well, that was safe enough. They don't have a problem with shoplifting from their displays: who's going to steal *one* shoe?

Then she went into the stationer's/wannabe bookshop where she looked at some exam-revision texts and pocketed a packet of gel pens. The counter assistant was busy, but Tony was floating about on the walkway. This time I'd get her. But as she left the shop and I tried to catch Tony's eye to make our arrest, he gave an almost imperceptible shake of his big head and walked on by. What the hell is going on?

*

I couldn't follow up my Mark Strain lead this afternoon due to my new arrangement with *him* that Thursday night is 'gourmet' night – i.e., I cook something that doesn't involve sausages, pizza or fish-fingers.

*

I've stopped going to the staff canteen as I'm trying to avoid Lindy-May until I have more news.

* * *

As of today, I've gone off hot-foam car-washes. That is because the perfectly sound car I drove on to the forecourt refused to start on completion of its ablutions. I've no knowledge whatsoever of the reasons why cars won't go, but the car-wash boss pretended to know for just long enough to get me shoved off his premises by his staff under the guise of 'getting you started'. I watched him sail down the road in my car with the two youngest children still in their booster seats, probably imagining themselves kidnapped.

When his young crew gave up pushing, it became clear that there was no life in my car, at which point he walked back to meet me scurrying towards him, handed me the keys and left me to my lonely fate. It could have been worse: we might have been stuck in the other car-wash, which is in the middle of nowhere; or the little bit of charge my elderly phone still held might have run out; or we might not have been AA members or had those bags of food shopping to keep us going.

As luck would have it, no sooner had everyone spent half an hour eating enough chocolate-chip cookies to spoil their evening meal, I tried the car again and it started. I phoned the AA to explain and went home. As luck would also have it, within minutes I had found a replacement passion for hot-foam car-washes: my new rubber bathmat. I cannot resist the smell of it. It's not a sexual thing, just deeply satisfying. I'm keeping the bathroom door closed so that every time I go in there it's full of the smell. (It's not harmful, like sniffing permanent marker pens.)

Because of the car-wash experience, I was unable to pursue my enquiries *re* Mark Strain.

* * *

Half-term has come round, and with it the first challenge to my new life–work balance. Eleanor and Terry have agreed to look after the children in the mornings, but strictly on a trial basis with the option to pull out if behaviour is bad. I've drummed into the children all the things I won't be able to buy them if I'm forced to give up my new job. I just hope they were listening.

*

In the end, we went out *en famille* for our Valentine's meal: Eleanor and Terry had already spent the morning with the children and I couldn't ask for the evening as well. We went to a place a bit out of town that's 'Under New Management'. The food and our children's behaviour were equally dire. Pizza shouldn't be bright orange. We wished we'd stayed at home and made toast.

Our middle child lifted the mood somewhat by telling us a little about the Zest for Life introduction-to-adolescence workshop he had attended last Friday with the other boys from his class. When we asked him what he'd found out he said his penis was going to get bigger, and when his older brother poured scorn on him for not knowing that already, he said he had but had never been told in the form of a word search before.

*

The children want to know why I was wrapping two egg boxes in brown paper.

*

Also, apparently every other child from school spent the entire half-term break in repeated visits to the newly opened Peter Piper's Soft Adventure Play Barn on the edge of town. Now I have to bring our children there.

* * *

I've found Mark Strain. He's not at the bottom of the canal. He's alive, if not very well, and staying with friends in the house where I met the surveyor.

How did I crack this case?

Easy. I wrapped up two egg boxes in brown paper and addressed the parcel to Mark Strain, care of the house I was staking out. I presented myself at the front door, posing as a neighbour who had taken in the parcel as a favour because, I claimed, the residents of the house had been out when the delivery van had called.

While the sixties-ish man who opened the door to me was reading the name and address and gratefully taking the parcel out of my hands, I stuck my foot on his hall mat so he couldn't shut me out. Then, I blurted that I was looking for Mark on behalf of his sister, Lindy-May Coulthard, who was beside herself with worry as she hadn't seen him for weeks and everyone she phoned denied having heard from him.

The last bit may have shamed him because he must have been one of those who had told Lindy-May they hadn't set eyes on Mark. He said this had gone on long enough and opened the door to let me in. (I had to make him promise that if I nipped back to my car to fetch my children, he wouldn't take the opportunity to lock me out. He assured me he wouldn't, and he was as good as his word.)

Mark Strain is nothing like Lindy-May. Not on the inside, anyway. Outwardly he's just as good-looking, and his smile is like hers, but while Lindy-May is constantly beaming and laughing, you get the feeling Mark's smile hasn't put in anything like as much mileage. Apart from the disappearance of her brother, Lindy-May bubbles with happiness. Mark does not.

To be honest, I think Brian and Sheelagh, Mark's hosts, were relieved I'd managed to find him. Seemingly he was in such distress when he arrived that they've scarcely been able to leave him on his own and certainly haven't been able to have anybody round. After nearly two months they're going stir-crazy. Plus, they were trying to sell their house when Mark threw himself on their mercy, and every time they've had a viewing they've had to hide him down the garden in the gazebo. When the surveyor came round last Wednesday, they left Mark there with his leather jacket on over his pyjamas and took themselves off for a much-needed walk.

I sensed that Brian and Sheelagh were glad to see three optimistic children and rewarded them with drinks and biscuits in the kitchen, which left me alone with Mark. He was still in his pyjamas, with a brown leather jacket over the top, and I did my best to respect this declaration of his unwellness, but I did ask him two things. First, I asked him if he could please phone Lindy-May: she had been so worried for so long. He looked ashamed and said that he would, now he was feeling better. And I asked if the things he was hiding from were on the outside or the inside.

He said the real problem was on the inside, but this made him unable to cope with ordinary outside things, including Tanya and Lindy-May. But he wasn't suffering from insurmountable debt, involved in a doomed love affair, or being threatened by hoodlums. It turned out that he suffers badly from anxiety, and sometimes it all gets too much. It also turned out that he used to have a Listening Angel, as I had, and that he had really missed her since the charity collapsed, as I had not, and that this hadn't helped with his most recent spell of panic and despair, which was now starting to lift.

Mark had hidden from Lindy-May because she is convinced that the answer to his anxiety lies in getting him out among people to take his mind off himself. In fact, this makes him feel like jumping out of an upper-storey window.

Tanya thinks he's just being weak and shouts at him. He fled to Brian and Sheelagh because they were the only people he could think of who might let him sleep on a camp-bed in their bedroom and keep a little night-light on, which he did for two weeks until he was able to sleep in a room on his own. Mark knew all along that the proper place for him was hospital, but he didn't think he could bear the regime. Brian and Sheelagh let him lie in bed watching *Neighbours* and old films for eight weeks, which seems to have done the trick. I didn't ask about medication, but I have my suspicions.

While we waited for the children to return from the kitchen, I confided that I, too, have had mental-health problems. I told Mark I was a recovering perfectionist or, as I've started to call it in my head, a recovering perfectionic, because it's just as painful and consuming a condition to live with as any other addiction. I was lucky to be diagnosed by Lucy, my therapist neighbour, who discovered that the total mess and chaos of my life and home were the result of trying to do everything perfectly or not at all. Mark was not dismissive of my confession. In fact, his eyes shone with sympathy, so I supplied some light conversation about how I'd met Lindy-May and how I was a store detective and didn't usually hunt for missing persons, and how my next mission was to do something about the posh girl thief, whom nobody seemed to want to nab. Mark wished me luck and told me to charge Lindy-May plenty for finding him. I felt embarrassed at the mention of my taking money for something that had been (a) so easy and now (b) so personal.

I didn't tell Mark that I, like him, have had grim episodes of anxiety because I was afraid of where that conversation might lead. He might have asked about my 'triggers', which include flying, lifts, going over bridges, going under bridges, enclosed spaces, travelling in flimsy cars, graveyards, hospital dramas, mice, rats, and more . . . I've heard that some people stuff their kettle spouts in case of germs. Although I don't do that, I'm a bit much with the hand-washing some days. I might have put ideas in his head that weren't already there, you see, and then he might have put ideas in mine. So I stayed mum. I've inherited my anxiety. It's in my genes. But I decided not to go into that, either.

As the children trotted back from the kitchen, Mark asked Sheelagh if he could use the phone, and a glance passed between them. It said this was an important moment for which they had been waiting. As I ushered the children out on to the pavement, I heard Mark say, just a little too brightly, 'Hello, Lin. It's me, Mark.'

* * *

Lindy-May has written me a cheque for £500. What for? A couple of afternoons spent visiting people, asking rather obvious questions and wrapping up two egg boxes in brown paper? I told her it was too much, but she insisted.

Do I have to declare this on my self-assessment tax return?

*

Karl from the juice bar (even he comes up to the canteen for his coffee – no wonder the juice bar's going belly-up) says the reason my car wouldn't start after the car-wash was water in the electrics. Whatever that means.

*

I had another hot flush in the kitchen tonight. *I'm too young for this.*

* * *

Mark Strain has left Brian and Sheelagh's so that they can move to the bungalow they've bought and has gone to stay with Lindy-May. She's delighted. Mark asked her if she would ask me to come round and see him again, so now Lindy-May has invited our family to her sort-of-ranch at the weekend. The children can see her horses, dogs and cats. *He* was surprisingly up for it. Is he perhaps a secret Lindy-May fan? Is he grateful for the £500? Or does he just like the idea of a day in the country? Actually, he and Lindy-May will probably get on like a house on fire: he enjoys confident people who talk a lot and can take being teased.

*

Nigel from Shoerama also cites 'water in the electrics' as the reason my car wouldn't start after being washed last week.

*

The posh girl thief was in the mall today. This time she was with a hair-flicking friend, but neither of them stole anything that I could see.

*

I bought chicken strips, red peppers and couscous with to-night's gourmet meal in mind. I also bought a new jar of Marmite, as the children will undoubtedly opt for sandwiches.

* * *

Oh dear. The local newspaper has printed the wrong names under the bonny-baby pictures, and furious parents have been in the Riverside shopping mall looking for someone to shout at. Apparently the newspaper is blaming the photographer for writing the wrong names on the backs of the photos, and the photographer is blaming the newspaper, saying everything was accurate when it left him. However, there's a £1,000 shopping voucher at stake, contributed to by the various outlets in the mall, so now the news is feeding back to their head offices and they're getting on the phone to Moira to say they don't want to be associated with a competition that's generating such dispute. I wouldn't like to be in Cheryl's shoes. It might not have been directly her fault but it was her 'baby'. Will Ted Twome provide a shoulder for her to cry on in her hour of need? (And other clichés.)

*

To make up for the fact that I'd left them with their grandparents all half-term, I took the children to Peter

Piper's Soft Adventure Play Barn after work today. It's still all shiny and new and doesn't yet have chewing gum stuck to the carpet. There's no upper age limit, but there is a height restriction. The male receptionist asked the children's ages, perhaps because our eldest looks and talks like the thirteen-year-old he is yet stands the height of an eleven-year-old. I lined him up against the height chart, to show we were legitimate, but the receptionist gave me a look that suggested I'd deliberately stunted my child's growth with specifically exploitative intent. He took their shoes with ill grace and we skulked into the main body of the barn.

As I drank my latte (£1.50!), I saw that the place was full of pregnant tummies and babies in car seats. With my young family now headed by a teenager, I had graduated from the changing-bag school without noticing. I no longer belonged. I was suddenly almost tearfully glad of my job, little and finite though it is. The children were moving forward, and so must I.

*

Peter Piper's Soft Adventure Play Barn has a couple of unlikely neighbours in a minicab firm and a cocktail lounge, all housed in the same prefabricated complex. As we were going to our car, whom should we see standing outside the cocktail lounge, in a denim shirt and jeans, clearly waiting for someone, but Ted Twome, deputy manager of the Riverside shopping mall. And whom did we see driving into the car park as we were driving out, in her cherry-red Honda Civic, but Cheryl, the Riverside's PR girl.

* * *

Lindy-May's house gleams at you in a way that can only be achieved by twice-weekly professional cleaning and no messy children. It's not all beige-and-gold bright like Tanya's flat – Lindy-May lets her dogs into the house – but the atmosphere and surfaces are evidently maintained by someone paid to do it.

When we arrived, Lindy-May seated us in the conservatory and sent the children, who had brought their Wellington boots, out to play with her dogs Jack and Dougal. Harry Ferris was already there, looking fairly resident in a large cane chair, trying to keep a marmalade cat off his cream trousers and drinking gin and tonic. Another woman was introduced as Hilary, Lindy-May's producer. And, of course, Mark was there, stroking a smoky cat that had jumped on to his knees and indicating his consequent inability to stand up to greet us. He was wearing the brown leather jacket, although the conservatory was quite warm.

All the adults had a few drinks, except Hilary and me, because we were driving, and *he* came right out of his shell, as he does in company, and had everyone laughing. Lindy-May kept turning to me and saying things like 'Where did you get him?' and 'Is he always like this?', which, of course, he isn't. As things have been going quite well between us recently, though, I just sat back and enjoyed the show, until Mark moved round to sit beside me and have a little private conversation under cover of the big noisy one.

He wanted to thank me for having found him and put him in touch with Lindy-May again. He had convinced himself that she had moved beyond worry for him into hatred, and I had turned up to tell him it was time and safe to call her. We talked a little about despair and how it eats your sanity but moved quickly on to the bonny-baby fiasco, which he seemed to enjoy, and the water-in-the-electrics-everyone's-suddenly-a-car-expert advice, which he said sounded reasonable enough to someone like him who'd never in his life looked under a bonnet in earnest.

We took a little walk out to the paddock where the children were 'training' the dogs to go over jumps made from old flowerpots and bamboo canes, and Mark said I was lucky, they were a gift, and I said I was and they were.

When we went back inside, Harry Ferris wanted to talk to Mark about racing, and Hilary cornered me to hear about how I'd tracked down Mark. What could I say? I'd found him in the first place I'd looked. Then she and I went into the kitchen and pulled all the stuff out of the fridge that Lindy-May's help had left covered with kitchen foil and cling film. We all sat round Lindy-May's enormous kitchen table and ate the food, then Lindy-May changed into a pair of jodhpurs and took the children to see the horses. Mark put a saddle on one and gave them each a turn walking round the paddock on a rein.

Once she's with her horses, Lindy-May calms right down. She stops being busy and noisy and is gentle, quiet and soothing. Which is the real her?

After he'd had a few more gin and tonics, Harry Ferris wanted to hear about my work as a store detective, but with a twinkle in his eye. He wanted to know if I had my own handcuffs, from which, I presume, I was to infer that he fantasised about using some on Lindy-May as a bedroom aid. I couldn't decide whether he was the most audacious flirt or simply a rather well-heeled old lecher. Lindy-May sat in his lap once or twice, in an adult kind of way.

As we were packing up the car to go, Mark said that if there was anything he could do for me, I was to let him know. So, without much hesitation, because we were leaving and there wasn't time for it, I told him there was one thing.

*

Lindy-May has asked us all to call her 'Lin' and *he* started to do it straight away and even the children managed it, but I find I can't. Why?

*

On second thoughts, I suspect Harry Ferris would fantasise about having the handcuffs used on him.

(I don't have any, by the way!)

*

If water got into the car's electrics during its wash, it could happen again at any time, couldn't it? Which means I really can't use car-washes again in case I get stuck just as badly or, even worse, in case the water does serious long-term damage. I'll have to concentrate on my bath-mat. What will I do when it runs out of smell? It can't last much longer. What else can I sniff that's made of rubber?

Could I get a swimming hat and keep it in a lunchbox?

* * *

This has been one of those days when I'd have been better off staying in bed. First, when I went to the canteen for my morning break, I overheard some of the supermarket girls tittering about 'something, something cardigan' and stopping abruptly when they saw me, only to give each other meaningfully repressed smiles. I knew they were talking about me, and I guessed what they were saying. The fact is, I don't have many clothes. I've my brown jeans, brown tops and brown cardigan, my black jeans, black tops and black-and-white cardigan, and I've been alternating them every few days. Until now, it hasn't mattered. I haven't been on show. But now that I've a job, people are noticing, and I need new clothes. Embarrassment always makes me sweat, too, so for the rest of the day I wasn't merely self-conscious about my attire but also about my odour.

Then, in the locker room at lunchtime, Moira Reynolds came storming at me with a clipboard. She tore off a piece of paper with a phone number on it, handed it to me and told me I was to ring Hilary, Lindy-May's producer, when I finished work. She also clarified that the office phone number was not for personal messages, and I could see that she hadn't liked being charged with such an errand. But it wasn't my fault! I didn't invite Hilary to ring! I wouldn't even have known Hilary if Moira didn't allow Lindy-May entry to our supposed-staff canteen, so Moira was the fraterniser, not me. Then Moira said, 'I believe you all had a good day, yesterday', and I realised she was jealous of my inclusion in Lindy-May's circle of friends. She shouldn't be. I don't even want to ring Hilary. I don't know what it's about, but I've a bad feeling I'm going to be asked to do something.

Next, the children listened keenly to the entire duration of Sandy Long's afternoon show on Zero FM because Lindy-May had told them she'd give Sandy their names and get a Ramones song dedicated to them on the air. There was no mention of the children or the Ramones.

And, as if these difficulties weren't enough, *he* brought home from work the news that *Go For It* magazine for self-employed small-business people, of which he's deputy editor, is merging with a similar title. He might lose his job. The only good thing about today was the cottage pie and peas I had in the staff canteen at lunchtime (90p).

* * *

Kathleen and Lorna have a few days off, because Fiona and Simon have taken the boys to see Fiona's parents in Scotland, so they called on me in the mall and asked if I'd like to meet up after work in Mumbles. At first I said I didn't know, because I'd have to find out from Eleanor if she could do my two o'clock school pick-up, but then Lorna produced a mobile and offered it to me to ring my mother. A mobile! When I first met Lorna she was barely brave enough to use the electronic cash register in the thrift shop where we worked! Now, seemingly, Fiona has supplied the 'grannies' with their own phone so they can ring up any time if there's a problem or a query with the children, and so they can take videos if Nathan or Samuel has a noteworthy 'first' experience or does something cute. As it happened, Eleanor was free, and I agreed to see my old friends for an hour.

*

Moira Reynolds has taken charge of salvaging the bonny-baby competition. She has given each of the misrepresented families a £25 voucher for Nursery World and negotiated with the local paper to start again. Cheryl, the PR girl, has been keeping a low profile.

*

I've played God. I've observed an episode of shoplifting and let the culprits go free. It happened in the sports shop. A straggly haired mother and her pustule-faced son were having a muted argument about a tracksuit top. It wasn't hard to make out that the one he wanted – felt he needed – was out of her price range. Again, she showed him the cheaper one. He was mortified even to look at it. Eventually, furtively, she stuffed the more expensive top into her supermarket carrier-bag. Furtively, he let her. She looked as if she had the weight of the world on her shoulders, and I let them go. Have I now, by omission, effectively stolen the price of the sweatshirt from my employers?

Well, maybe I wasn't a hundred per cent sure I saw her put the sweatshirt in her bag.

*

Four pounds ninety-five for a panini with salad! One pound seventy for a milky coffee! I'd forgotten the price of things in the commercial sector. I had a good chat with Kathleen and Lorna, though. They're getting on well sharing Kathleen's bungalow. Kathleen does all their ironing, which she quite likes, and Lorna cleans the grate and lays the fire. They share the cooking. When I asked about Kathleen's husband, who was discharged from hospital some time ago and placed in a nursing-home, I thought Kathleen was defensively quick to answer. Seemingly, Walter is still unable to get in and out of bed by himself and can't walk very well, so he isn't ready to come home yet, but Kathleen dutifully visits him twice a week, bringing him puzzle books and cinnamon lozenges. Walter's laundry is done in the home, but Kathleen finds it hard to accept that they merely tumble-dry his pyjamas and don't bother to iron them.

Meanwhile, she and Lorna are loving being Happy Grannies. Nathan and Samuel are the sort of children who eat whatever is put in front of them and take an afternoon nap at the same time each day without getting cranky. Apparently, they're a pleasure to look after. Fiona and Simon were less than enthusiastic about Kathleen and Lorna having entered the boys in the bonny-baby competition without asking their permission, but once they saw the hillbilly pictures in the newspaper they were won over. (How wrong I was.) However, they do not believe in buying extra papers so they can multiple-vote: they think this undermines the nature of the competition. If Nathan or Samuel wins, their parents want them to do so on merit. (Don't they realise that the other parents are buying up fifty and a hundred copies, at 95p a voting form, as their stake in a £1,000 prize? It's better odds than scratch cards.)

*

The radio was still tuned to Zero FM from yesterday, so while I was getting our meal ready I heard Sandy Long's dedication to the children, even though they missed it. (This was lucky, as Sandy Long didn't play anything like the Ramones. He played 'The Piña Colada Song', which they'd have despised.)

*

It's the Parents' Committee meeting tomorrow. I must phone Mark.

* * *

Today, I saw the posh girl thief again. She was talking to Leon, swaying about elegantly on her nimble feet and playing coquettishly with her bottle of mineral water. Is she Leon's girlfriend, or aspiring girlfriend? Is this why he and Tony turn a blind eye? And is she the only thief going about her robbing business undisturbed? Or are they all at it? Is there some tacit understanding that thieving opportunities for one's loved ones are a perk of working in this place?

No. I can't believe that. But when the posh girl left Leon, I didn't bother following her. What would have been the point?

*

Tonight, it was the monthly meeting of the Parents' Committee. I felt successful and well organised because, thanks to Mark Strain, I was able to hand over a sealed envelope containing sixteen rounds of six questions for the Spring Quiz. I didn't pretend I'd written them myself, because I want to be able to compete on the night, but I assured the group they had come from a most reliable source. And Mark is reliable, in his own way. He might be susceptible to complete emotional breakdown from time to time, but his judgement is sound enough and, as he had nothing else on, inventing questions was sort of occupational therapy for him.

But I really impressed them when it came to discussing the summer fête. This is the biggest event of our year and therefore the one into which we put most work. To maximise the returns, though, we need a huge turnout, and the last couple of times that hadn't happened. So, somebody suggested we get a celebrity to open it, but somebody else said that would cost us a fortune – we needed to be raising money, not spending it. Everybody sort of agreed with both suggestions – they fancied the idea of a celebrity but didn't want to fork out an appearance fee.

I said I might be able to get Lindy-May Coulthard, from *The Lindy-May Morning Show*, for nothing, and everybody went quiet. I sat there, blushing, wondering if I'd made a complete fool of myself for suggesting that anyone from our local radio station could be described as a 'celebrity', but then Caroline, our secretary, said, 'Could you?'

I said it depended on Lindy-May having no prior engagements but, yes, I thought there was a distinct possibility, and everybody sort of purred. Then I knew I had proposed a good idea, not a stinker, and Caroline wrote it down as an action point with my initials beside it. There was a bit more fête chat about bouncy castles, nail art and tombola prizes, and a quick review of the playground-parent scheme, which has been a distinguished success, and a little bit of gossip about the new year-three teacher and what they had supposedly said about her at her last school, and some speculation that Marilyn Softly is returning to teach special needs, and then it was time for home.

Caroline kept the questions sealed in their envelope as she, too, wanted to compete in the quiz. She's going to hand them over to the principal, whom she hopes will fulfil the role of question master on the night.

*

All the staff at *Go For It* have been called to a meeting tomorrow afternoon. *He* has a bad feeling about it.

* * *

Today, Kathleen and Lorna, with their young charges, were back in the Riverside shopping mall. They sat at the bistro tables outside the gourmet coffee place where they had bought decaff babyccinos for Nathan and Samuel. The grannies were excited because the boys are going to stay overnight with them for the first time. Fiona and Simon are having a man in to do some work on the house, and they don't want a lot of dust round the little ones. I thought of our tatty place with its chipped paint and ancient carpets installed by the previous owners. Don't talk to me about dust. If *he* loses his job now we will never be able to make our home nice.

I asked Kathleen what sort of work Fiona and Simon are having done, and she said they were having their hall floor tiled, only Fiona and Simon don't call it a hall, they call it a *vestibule*. I offered to lend the grannies our old travel cot, which is still immaculate, but instead of proving helpful, this seemed to cause them worry in case Fiona and Simon weren't keen on borrowed items. Good grief. Kathleen asked me what the difference was between a hall and a vestibule. I thought, The people who own it, Kathleen, but I said I didn't know.

*

He is very, very late home from work tonight. My gourmet efforts ended up under tin foil in the fridge. (Usually a holding-station for the bin.) It must have been a hell of a meeting.

* * *

As we were all sitting in the canteen today, choosing our favourites from the bonny-baby competition (re-run with accuracy in this week's local paper), Lindy-May swept in to join us. While she peered at the double-page spread of baby pictures, I summoned my courage and broached the subject of her possibly opening our summer fête at school. (For nothing.) She sighed, which was not encouraging, then explained she would have to consult her agent.

I immediately felt stupid. Of course Lindy-May couldn't do something like open a school fête at the drop of a hat. Of course she would have a diary of engagements and contracts and things. She was probably sighing over requests like this all the time. But in the moment it had taken me to berate myself, Lindy-May had flipped open her little phone and speed-dialled Phyllis, her agent and, in no time at all, had asked Phyllis how she, Lindy-May, was fixed for 'doing a freebie on Friday 1 June'. 'At what time?' Lindy-May asked me, putting me on the spot. I guessed: one p.m.? Lindy-May relayed this into her phone, said 'Right' and 'OK' to Phyllis a few times, asked something about Harry Ferris and said 'Leave that to me.' Then she said some other stuff about Hilary her producer, something about that being 'Hilary's baby', followed by a laugh – for which I guess you'd have needed the other half of the conversation to make sense of it. Then she rang off. The upshot is, Lindy-May and Harry Ferris are both coming to open our school fête! I can hardly wait to tell them at school.

*

Lindy-May told me not to put off ringing Hilary. She says it's nothing for me to worry about and may be to my advantage. But Lindy-May has no inkling of the range and depth of things that worry me.

*

No immediate redundancies are to follow the merging of *Go For It* with the other trade journal for small businesses, but staff were told at last night's meeting that an independent time-and-motion person is coming in next week to start assessing who does what before deciding who's for the chop. (They didn't admit that last bit, but everyone has worked it out.) This could be bad news for *him*: although he has always worked very hard, all his tasks are now duplicates of the same tasks done at the other title, and there's no way anyone's going to continue paying two people to do the same job. His opposite number is called Jeremy, who is apparently acting nonchalant, which makes him think that Jeremy already knows his job is safe, which means his isn't, and that is more than a tad worrying.

*

Kathleen and Lorna were back in today with the boys, looking somewhat haggard. They'd had a tough night with

Nathan and Samuel, who had found it hard to sleep away from their own beds. They'd wanted to bunk in with Kathleen and Lorna and weren't happy that Kathleen and Lorna slept in different beds, as they'd wanted to snuggle down between them. After much crying, story-telling and drinks of water, Kathleen and Lorna gave in and got into Kathleen and Walter's marital bed with the boys. They spent what was left of the night clinging to opposite edges of the mattress, trying not to fall out on to the floor, while Nathan and Samuel sprawled contentedly in the centre.

Exhausted from the night's exploits, the grannies had then decided to take the boys to Peter Piper's Soft Adventure Play Barn, where they could relax over a cup of coffee and a muffin while the youngsters expended some energy, rolling and tumbling. Unfortunately Nathan clashed heads with another small boy on the bouncy castle and somebody threw balls from the ball-pit directly at Samuel's face, which made them cry. Kathleen and Lorna didn't even get to drink their coffee but ended up having to send Fiona a picture of the injuries via their mobile phone.

*

Our children, who only sleep with us if they've nightmares, have proposed the theory that Arthur was able to pull Excalibur from the stone because the previous efforts had loosened it. They may have a point.

* * *

Mark phoned this evening to let me know that a new crime drama is starting tonight, by the same writer as the *Mac* series. I already knew this, but I was glad he'd thought of me. He asked how things were going on the crime front locally with shoplifters and I told him it had been a quiet week. He asked if I had got to the bottom of the posh girl mystery and I admitted I hadn't. I suspected there was a whole can of worms behind her – but was I prepared to open it? I asked Mark if he was still living at Lindy-May's, and he said he was. He also said that Brian and Sheelagh have accepted an offer well over the asking price on their house. I asked if, ultimately, he was aiming to return to his and Tanya's apartment by the canal, and he said no. It's only rented, and he's told Tanya he'll pay for the next six months to give her time to find somewhere else, but they won't be getting back together.

I wonder what Mark's financial circumstances are that he can afford to pay six months' rent on an apartment he doesn't live in at a time when he doesn't have any obvious source of income. I don't want to come right out and ask him, but I might fish a little the next time I see Lindy-May.

Mark and I had our customary sharing of thoughts on the anxiety front. We have a little codename for it now. We call it 'water in the electrics.' Luckily, we're both pretty well dried out at the moment, but you never can tell when you're in for another drenching.

I confided in Mark about Terry, my father, whom I

regard as the conduit of my water-in-the-electrics gene. It turns out Mark has read my father's poetry books, so he wasn't at all surprised to learn that Terry is a sufferer, but he has also read Terry's zany poems for children, which show my father in a different light. (I owe those children's poems a lot: thanks to their sitting second only to Roald Dahl throughout much of the 1980s, I was granted everything from inclusion in the school ski-trip to the deposit on my first house!) I must say, when it comes to discussing the possibility of inter-generational anxiety, Mark comes over a bit reticent. I don't think he really buys it.

As I was on the telephone anyway, I finally rang Hilary. She was still at the studios, although it was after seven. I had known all along that she was going to ask me to do something, and I was right. The thing is, Hilary is insisting that the thing she's asking me to do is straightforward, but I know it isn't. The other thing is, she's prepared to pay me well, and with *his* job being in jeopardy, we might need the money.

Part Two

Baby

As I was combing my hair in the staff locker area this morning, Moira Reynolds popped in to ask if I'd come to her office before starting work. Ever the overgrown school-child, I naturally thought I was in trouble and was immed-iately racking my brain for what I'd done wrong.

I needn't have worried. It turned out that now I've been a member of staff at the Riverside shopping mall for a whole month, I've qualified for a clutch of benefits. Moira handed me a bundle of coupons for free juice at the juice bar, money off in the sports shop and the discount jeweller's, plus a laminated card that gets me ten per cent off everything in the supermarket, Nursery World and Shoerama. On top of this, I can join the mall's corporate-membership scheme at the gym in the leisure centre, I can book appointments with the subsidised in-house hairdresser – I'd wondered how the checkout girls always managed to look so coiffed – and I can get my fees paid if I go on a computer-literacy course. I also get to join in the staff training sessions on Thursday mornings.

At my tea break, I asked Brenda where I could find the in-house hairdresser, and it turns out that she's next door to the staff canteen. (From this information I was able to deduce that the bad-egg smell is not from the canteen's cooking but from hair-perming solution. I can take a holiday from my usual tuna lunchtime snack and try the egg mayonnaise.) I ventured shyly into the salon and was lucky to slot into someone else's cancelled appointment for Friday afternoon. Friday night is the Spring Quiz.

*

I saw Jill looking at the displays in Shoerama. Why? Shoerama specialises in 'man-made soles, man-made uppers' and has nasty thin carrier-bags. The shoes in Jill's place are things of beauty, and she has gorgeous, sleek black bags with gold writing. So, does professional curiosity bring her here, or is she like a man who can't resist taking a trip through a red-light district, even though he has a beautiful wife at home?

*

I looked in the local pages of the *Radio Times* to see what they'd said about the programmes on Zero FM. On Harry Ferris's show: 'Irreverent chat and banter with Harry and the usual suspects.' On Lindy-May: 'Topical chat, news and the

Coffee Break Quiz.' And on Sandy Long: 'Your dedications and requests, with news on the hour.' Not exactly overwhelmingly compelling, but Zero FM is one of the most successful regional commercial stations around. How come?

*

The time-and-motion person began his work at *Go For It* yesterday. *He* arrived in work at his usual time to find that practically everybody else had shown up early to make a good impression, which made it appear that he had rolled in late. He said the first three tasks he set about doing turned out to have been done already by Jeremy, so he reckons he's definitely going to be sacked as a waste of space. Last night, he looked up statutory redundancy payment on the computer. He says that when the amount is set beside the rearing and possible higher education of three children, plus the desire to ward off poverty in old age, it's practically invisible. I'm used to us being poor, but I hadn't thought before of it persisting when we're elderly and have no future to look forward to.

I thought of Hilary's proposal again and her hint that, if I do a good job on her assignment, there might be a permanent post for me. Although it alarms me, I don't think I can afford to turn it down.

* * *

I caught another shoplifter this morning. It was a little like the pram scam, only this time with handbags. The culprit was a respectable-looking woman in a spring coat with zip-up green boots and, most likely, wouldn't have caught my eye were it not for her cowboyish gait. Then I noticed that, unusually, she wasn't carrying a reasonable-sized handbag, like most women do, but a compact little thing that wasn't much more than a purse. I followed her, as surreptitiously as I could, until she stopped at the bags stand. I paused nearby, at the belts. Innocent until proven guilty, she might have been in the process of choosing a new handbag to buy. Perhaps the strap on the old one had broken – that's happened to me – and she had been left with the purse thing. But when she popped the purse inside one of the display bags, my suspicions were aroused, and when she slid a little pair of nail-clippers out of her coat pocket and snipped off the label, I had to think the worst. A glance at the walkway told me Leon was right by the doors so I knew I had her. I matched her cowboy strides until she stepped out of the supermarket, and I indicated to Leon to block her way.

She was the most indignant thief I'd caught yet. She kept trilling, 'I'm a civil servant, you know. I'm a civil servant,' and 'my lawyer will have something to say about this.' When Moira and Ted came down, they were unable to persuade her to accompany them upstairs in the staff-and-goods lift, like most people do, so instead they and Leon had to stand there at the front door with her, waiting for the police. Moira thanked me for my efforts – although I bet she was thinking this one was more bother than she was worth – and told me to go back about my business.

As I walked away, the civil servant called, 'You'll be sorry, you little bitch.' It was my worst experience of store detection so far.

*

The two-part crime drama wasn't bad. The writing was sharp enough, and it was well acted, but the whodunnit element was undermined by the appearance in the cast list of a top actress who didn't play a detective and didn't play the victim and who, it could therefore be surmised, as she hadn't taken the job for a walk-on part, *must* be the murderer, which she was. Don't casting directors think of these things?

* * *

I attended my first staff-training session this morning. It lasts thirty minutes and is for all the centre staff except Brenda, who can still sell fags and newspapers at the front of the supermarket when the rest is shuttered off, and either Leon or Tony. They advise thwarted shoppers of our nine to nine-thirty closure for staff training every Thursday and invite them to sit on the seats by the grabber machines until we troop down from upstairs.

This morning's session was led by a well-upholstered woman in a drapey, crêpey two-piece and well-crowned front teeth. She gave a sort of lecture on customer services and particularly on the importance of asking 'open' questions.

When you boiled it right down, she told everybody to stop asking, 'Can I help you?' and start asking, '*How* can I help you?' It was a bit wasted on me, as I'm meant to be incognito among the shoppers. Still, it was a change. Somebody said the woman was a 'corporate trainer' and, as such, earned £300 an hour. Can this be right? For changing 'Can I help you?' to '*How* can I help you?'

*

Mark Strain is an antiques and collectibles dealer with a shop in an old steading in a picturesque village about two miles north of our town. He's hoping to reopen on Monday. Lindy-May thinks he should renovate the adjoining bit of steading and open a coffee shop for his customers. She says the right catering manager could do all the work, and it would draw more people out to make a day of it, but Mark is an enthusiast rather than an entrepreneur and doesn't want to enter the world of chicken-and-vegetable bake and side orders of garlic potatoes; he prefers art-deco bedroom furniture and silver Victorian serving spoons. He doesn't even open his shop until after lunch because he says people don't shop for antiques in the mornings, and I'm sure he's right. He says his clientele are mainly honeymooners and retired people, and they don't have to get up early.

I learned all this over lunch in the canteen with Lindy-May (egg mayonnaise on brown bread with a sprig of parsley, 40p), who, I think, makes it a policy to be open (indiscreet). I say this because she told me not only about

Mark's business – which she says does extremely well and will continue to do so even having been closed for so long because he has a terrific eye for what sells and is an inadvertently brilliant salesman – but also that Mark probably doesn't need to work as their wealthy parents left him most of their estate. Seemingly, they were the sort of old-fashioned people who believed that a man needed the means to look after a family while their daughter would be provided for by her husband.

Lindy-May explained this without a trace of bitterness – she's big on honouring her beloved parents' best-intended wishes, plus she adores Mark. Of course, she's hardly broke. Her first husband was the equestrian godfather Jimmy Coulthard and, in addition to her job at Zero FM, she can command a £500 appearance fee for presenting prizes at awards ceremonies or opening new restaurants. This is the sort of thing she just throws out while she's sipping her cappuccino.

Harry Ferris gets £1,000!

*

He went to work early this morning to get in before horrible Jeremy. Typical of his luck just now, the time-and-motion person didn't come in at all today. He says he doesn't know if he'll be able to make it to the quiz night tomorrow as he's not going to leave the office any more until after Jeremy does if the time-and-motion person is about, and this will take as long as it takes. I've tried suggesting that perhaps quality of effort rather than quantity of hours will impress the time-and-motion man more, but this didn't go down well. He ranted that he's not an ideas man, he never has been, and that he's always survived by putting in the hours, working hard and seeing the job's done properly.

*

I looked at the local pages of the *Radio Times* again to see what new things they'd find to say about the Zero FM schedule for today. On Harry Ferris: 'Harry and his crew engage the public with their irreverent humour, plus tunes.' On Lindy-May: 'Who will be the lucky winner of Lindy-May's star prize in this morning's Coffee Break Quiz?' And on Sandy Long: 'Sandy keeps the music coming, with news and traffic updates on the hour.'

I say, 'How inane can you get?' Who writes this stuff?

*

Some of the checkout girls were saying that a new reiki healer has opened for business on Park Street – the one with all the architects and dentists where Brian and Sheelagh lived when they were looking after Mark. They are debating whether to go for a reiki session or to a fortune-teller.

I'd advise the fortune-teller, but this might be because the last reiki healer I got involved with temporarily stole my husband. Her name was Prentiss Prine, an American, and she started out as my Listening Angel, a sort of friendship service offered to the lonely and anxious by the Listening

Angels' Trust, in whose charity shop I eventually worked. Even though I know Prentiss has returned to her flamboyantly dysfunctional family in the States, I won't be a hundred per cent happy until I've checked out the details of this new practice and ascertained for definite that it isn't her.

*

Today, I looked longingly at the small queue in the Suds Bros car-wash as I drove past, but I didn't go in.

*

I've no one to form a quiz team with tomorrow.

* * *

Our son has a new girlfriend. He says he singled her out for her exceptional kindness to him. I wish they could marry immediately, before his head is turned by some heartless lovely with large breasts, as kindness is the exact number-one personal quality I desire in his chosen life partner. Unfortunately, my dream of hasty wedlock cannot be as they are only six.

*

Kathleen and Lorna came into the Riverside shopping mall in a frenzy of excitement because Nathan has won the first weekly heat of the bonny-baby competition. I looked at the picture, reprinted in this week's issue with a rosette in the top corner, and I've to admit that, with his big blue eyes and chestnut curls, he's a good-looking child. Poor little Samuel is somewhat less prepossessing. His eyes are a more insipid blue, and his hair thin and mousy. Will this difference blight their growing up? Will the girls queue up for Nathan and ignore Samuel? How do Fiona and Simon deal with having one remarkably – competition-winningly – good-looking child and one non-runner? Do parents notice? (Is any of *our* children much more gorgeous than the others? Have I ever really looked?) Is either Fiona or Simon a good-looker and the other not? Although I feel I know them, I've never actually met them. I may ask Kathleen and Lorna about this.

Anyhow, I told the grannies about the Parents' Committee's Spring Quiz being on tonight, how *he* was probably having to work late and I was unhappy to walk in team-less and on my own, how disappointed I was at missing the chance to test my brain in a social situation that sounded as if it might be fun. Kathleen told me they have quizzes sometimes in Walter's nursing-home and that sometimes Walter's team wins. She said they do well because they've a retired schoolmaster who remembers everything that ever happened in the world up to about 1975, when his memory stops, and they've Walter: he has to walk with a frame but there's nothing wrong with his mental faculties and he reads the *Daily Mail* every morning in his bedroom chair.

*

Moira Reynolds joined me at my morning break. She said the editor of the local newspaper is thrilled with the success of the bonny-baby competition. People are buying papers in droves for the enclosed voting slip. He wanted to sound her out about making it an annual thing. Moira's not sure. The competition generates weeks of interest in the newspaper, as they print each heat, but we in the mall had only a few hectic days while the photographer was *in situ*. I told Moira that I knew the winner of the first heat, which initially caused her nepotism concerns but only until I explained that I'd never met his parents and that he comes into the mall quite often with my friends, his surrogate grannies. Then she relaxed and told me with pride that her daughter, Penny, had correctly forecast Nathan as the winner from last week's photographs.

She also said that the civil-servant shoplifter is kicking up a fuss. She told the police that when she left the supermarket she wasn't trying to steal the handbag but was merely looking for a mirror in which to see herself with it. She also said that she cut the shop labels off the bag by mistake and was aiming for a plucked thread on her coat. All the previous shoplifters I've caught have cooperated with the proceedings and I haven't had to do more than type out a short statement on Moira's computer for use in the courts. Moira says this one is definitely going to contest the charge, and it's up to her, Moira, and Ted Twome to decide whether to press ahead or let it go. It's tempting to let it go, just for a quiet life, but then the civil servant might turn the tables and try to do the mall for wrongfully apprehending her and holding her in full view of a busy shopping centre while awaiting the police. It isn't the first time Moira has dealt with a situation like this, and she says the woman might be a civil servant but that she has 'compensation culture' written all over her.

*

What with probably not being able to go to the quiz and the stuff about the civil-servant shoplifter playing on my mind, I was delighted when Lindy-May turned up bright and bubbly in the canteen at lunchtime. She thought I was a bit subdued, and when I told her why, she said she'd go to the quiz with me! Not only that, but she whipped out her little mobile and phoned Harry Ferris, who was still at the station editing a special for St Patrick's Day, and he said he'd come, too. Before I'd finished my lasagne and green salad (£1.10), Lindy-May's mobile had trilled, and this time it was Sandy Long to ask if he could join us because it sounded like a laugh.

Three Zero FM presenters all free on a Friday night! I could hardly believe it. I was touched and tearful that Lindy-May had solved my problem – and how! Lindy-May said it was possible only because it was March, a lean spell for awards-ceremony dinners, which tended to come at end-of-season, in May and June, and it just so happened that no new restaurants were opening this Friday. I was simply glad I had a team.

Of course, what happened next was that, as I was walking through the mall on my way home, I bumped into Kathleen and Lorna again, coming out of Pharmacity where they had been buying a large tub of E45 cream to protect Walter from bedsores. They looked pleased to see me and said they'd been going to ring me if they hadn't found me. They'd talked it over and were willing to be my quiz team. Well, of course I couldn't tell them I no longer needed them – they looked so pleased – so I thanked them and told them what time to meet me at the venue. Thank goodness the Parents' Committee decided on teams of up to eight. I'll just have to explain to everybody when we get there.

*

The in-house hair salon is a cosy little set-up. Janice, the stylist, is so comfortable in her domain that she goes about in her slippers. Her apprentice is her niece, Jodie, who confided that she would prefer to be working in one of the funky salons in the town centre (where everybody wears black and nobody smiles at you), but she applied too late for hairdressing college and is biding her time with her auntie Janice until she can apply again. Jodie washes the hair, sweeps up the cuttings and makes the tea and coffee. Janice does the cutting, perming, colouring and blow-drying. They're both kept busy.

I used to fear the hairdressers' back-washes because I had heard on daytime TV about 'beauty-parlour stroke' where people had a mini-stroke with their head back over the basin and walked out of the salon numb down one side and unable to remember where they'd parked the car. Sometimes I've felt that the weight of my head would break my neck, but not at Janice's. I predict that Jodie will one day be a great hairdresser, because she adjusts the washbasin to just the right height before applying any pressure. She doesn't say much, but that's OK with me. I like a bit of quiet. Janice is just the opposite. She talks non-stop, and that's OK, too, because she's so competent at keeping the flow going that it's no strain on me.

Janice loves being the in-house hairdresser because she's so affordable to ordinary working women, because of all the discounts and corporate benefits she receives (she's on the same package as me) and because she has almost the same freedoms she would if she worked for herself but without the pressure of having to turn a profit. She also made sure I knew she doesn't like people to make appointments for their lunch-breaks, as they inevitably return to work malnourished and – if she's a little bit behind – late. She prefers to take part-timers, like me, well before or just after their shifts, and full-timers on their day off.

*

We won the quiz! Harry, Lindy-May, Sandy Long, Kathleen, Lorna, *he* and I! We won eight bottles of wine between us. The runners-up got four, and the two teams that tied for third place got two each. Sandy Long enjoyed it so much he wanted to know if there'd be another soon so we could do it again.

He was quite good. He didn't have a particular field of knowledge like Lindy-May, who was very well informed on

Olympic sports, or Harry, who was excellent on geography, but he knew bits and pieces about 1970s TV shows and the Eurovision Song Contest. I knew a bit about books, authors and telly, and *he* knew about football and rugby. Kathleen and Lorna didn't seem to know much at all but made a good show of confirming the rightness of answers once other people had suggested them. (Kathleen and Lorna were acting weird. Every time any of the Zero FM people spoke to them, they answered in fake, telephone voices.) The general consensus was that the quiz had been fair, and we won by six clear points. (I wonder if the runners-up would have minded had they had known that the brother of one of our team had written the questions.)

Suddenly, I'm the centre of attention because I had three Zero FM presenters on my team. I suppose I'd have to concede that Harry has a sort of magnetism, but, as he's already involved with Lindy-May, not to mention his wife, I don't look at him in that way. You should have seen how everybody just dropped over to our table to chat to me. There were people I've been shyly helloing at for years who could hardly be bothered to acknowledge my existence, and suddenly, lo and behold, there they were by my side, asking about the children, the school parking mayhem, anything that would allow them to hover within sniffing distance of the Zero FM gang for a little while.

Harry Ferris flirted with pretty much everyone, males included. I think he likes to cultivate an image of being open to anything. Meanwhile, Lindy-May just sat back and let him. I think she reckons that, even if he were to go for someone younger, say, with long blonde hair instead of grey and spiky, he won't find anyone who's quite as much fun as her, and she's probably right.

Harry Ferris drank gin and tonic. Lindy-May drank white-wine spritzer. Sandy Long drank rum and Coke and ate Scampi Fries. Kathleen and Lorna each drank one Tia Maria, then opted for orange juice. *He* and I drank red wine.

When the photographer from the local newspaper came, Caroline, the secretary of the Parents' Committee, told me to ask Lindy-May, Harry and Sandy if they'd mind being in the picture, so they ended up standing against the wall with Caroline and the school principal, smiling for the camera. I suppose this happens to them a lot. Lindy-May was also asked to draw the raffle, which meant that when she pulled out Harry's winning ticket (he *had* bought twenty quid's worth), she felt obliged to put it back. Harry looked quite sick to miss out on the first prize of a bottle of Martell cognac.

Then, when it was time to go, we discovered that only one minicab had been ordered. (By me.) Harry told me to take Kathleen and Lorna in our cab and he would order another for him, Lindy-May and Sandy. I said he'd have to wait ages as it was throwing-out time on a Friday night. Lindy-May smiled and said Harry never had to wait long because all the drivers loved to be able to say they'd had him in their cab.

Then she suggested we all went to my house for a nightcap or coffee, and my heart lurched. It's all right for people like her, whose homes are dependably clean and tidy except, perhaps, for some new tooth marks made by the dogs. But I was picturing ours – the dishevelled sofa cushions, the ashy grate, the crumby carpet and trails of inside-out clothing left by the children. But, like the angels they are and because their bungalow was nearer, Kathleen suggested we go to her and Lorna.

They were utterly *thrilled* when everybody said yes. They made instant coffee in a vacuum jug and served it in the front room with home-made ginger cake and shortbread. Harry Ferris was so enthusiastic about the ginger cake that Kathleen wrapped up the leftovers in tin foil and gave them to him to take home. She's going to bake him one of his own and give it to me to give to Lindy-May to pass on.

We didn't stay late. Kathleen and Lorna had made it known earlier that they were looking after Nathan and Samuel in the morning while Fiona and Simon go clothes shopping, and *he* and I had Eleanor and Terry sitting in our front room waiting to get home, so we had all booked the minicabs to return for us in an hour. When we left, Lindy-May still looked as fresh as a daisy. She kissed us goodnight, then linked arms with Harry and Sandy to march down the driveway and into their cab.

Lindy-May mentioned the project Hilary wants me to work on. She says Hilary is tired of doing middle-of-the-road programmes like hers and is dying to get her teeth into something meatier. The programme she wants me to help her with is a pilot, at this stage, but she hopes it'll be sufficiently successful to launch a proper series. It's about finding people who have gone missing, and I'm to be employed as a freelance researcher, although really it sounded more like I'm going to be a detective. Hilary picked me because I'd found Mark. She refuses to understand that I did it almost completely by luck. If we didn't need the money, I wouldn't even contemplate taking it on. But we do need the money.

In the pilot, the person we're searching for is the mother of a baby abandoned thirty-five years ago in our town. Hugh, the baby – now a grown man obviously – was brought up by an adoptive family in Wales, and he has no complaints about that. He was very happy. But ever since he has known about the adoption, he has wanted to find out about his birth parents, and ever since he learned he was a foundling, he has wondered how he could trace them.

He wrote to various people for help, and one of his letters found its way to Hilary, who was looking for a new challenge. She agreed to make the pilot programme based on his search. I'm not a nosy-parker by nature. I don't want to go poking about in other people's lives. But, then, it's Hugh's life too, and he's asked for our help.

*

108

Didn't catch any thieves today. Michelle is still high-fiving me every lunchtime by the staff-and-goods lift.

* * *

A row has kicked off at *Go For It*, now incorporating *Self-Starters' Monthly*. It began when horrible Jeremy took it upon himself to instigate a new double-page-spread feature, 'Self-Starter of the Month', and devised a special block to head the page, using his own picture by-line. *He* was ripping mad when he found out about it because, let's face it, a lot of what filled the pages of *Go For It* had always been profile material – that and news about new training or funding initiatives and top tips on tax. Now Jeremy was claiming paramount status for whatever big profile he chose to do each month, leaving the rest of them to make as much as they could of what remained. So, *he*, already on a short fuse because of the time-and-motion person observing him, kicked up a bit of a fuss to the two amalgamated editors, and Jeremy did his nonchalant thing again and said, no problem, let *him* do the Self-Starter of the Month profile this time, and let it be *his* picture by-line at the top of the page because the last thing he, Jeremy, wanted to do was tramp on anybody's toes. So now *he*'s in a worse tizz than ever because, having made a stand, he feels he has to come up with somebody really good to profile, and with only three days to the deadline, he can't think of anyone suitable.

I asked who Jeremy had been planning to profile, and it turns out he's already done the interview, with a flourishing country blacksmith, which sounds pretty interesting. Desperate to help, I suggested the new reiki healer, but *he* said the world of self-employment is utterly saturated with middle-aged, born-again reflexologists, colour therapists and hot-stones applicants, and if he has to speak to just one more New Age holistic type he'll have to put his head in a bucket. But when I thought about it again and suggested self-employed antiques and collectibles dealer Mark Strain, he said, 'Yes! That's brilliant', and kissed me where we were standing, beside the sink.

At the minute, his magazine is in the crazy situation of having two editors and two deputies, and each editor looks out for his own 'boy' and vice versa. But the situation cannot continue. One of each is going to have to go or be demoted. The question is, who?

*

The Riverside shopping mall's general handyman was on the walkway today, putting up signs saying, 'Store Detectives Operating in These Premises.' I felt quite important.

* * *

The civil-servant shoplifter has phoned the manager of the Riverside shopping mall and asked for my name so that she can make a written complaint against me. Why me? My involvement with her lasted about two minutes, while Leon, Ted Twome and Moira stood with her for a quarter of an hour! I'm feeling a little paranoid. Ted Twome and Moira have both mentioned the matter to me and have assured me that the mall will not be giving out my name and that I've nothing to worry about from this odd woman because I was simply doing my job. All the same, I keep wondering. Why is she picking on me?

*

Kathleen and Lorna called on me at work to leave in the ginger cake for Harry. I put it in the empty shopping-bag I carry and promised to stick a Post-it note to it and leave it in the canteen for collection by Lindy-May. Kathleen and Lorna looked dubious, as if a staff canteen was a dangerous place to leave a cake unattended, but I reasoned with them that no one would dare tamper with or steal goods belonging to a store detective – which seemed to reassure them.

*

He phoned Mark Strain, who agreed to do the profile interview even though he loathes talking about himself and will hate every minute of it. The state *he*'s in over work matters, he doesn't care if Mark likes it or not.

*

A flyer has come through our letterbox from the Millennium Exhibition and Arts Centre. It reads, 'Women. Still holding out for a hero? Stop! Try finding your inner shero!' At first I thought it said, 'Find your inner stereo', which left me puzzled. But then I got it. *He*-ro, *She*-ro. Good grief.

* * *

Lorcan Hinds is staying at Bruce Willis's house in Hollywood. It said so in the complimentary newspaper I read in the canteen on my morning break. The same report also said that 'Hinds' had been seen 'carousing' with Welsh expatriate actor Anthony Hopkins and his fellow countryman Tom Jones, and that 'Hinds' was linked to British actress Beth Marsh, who had also recently stayed *chez* Willis. But I'm sure I've read that Anthony Hopkins doesn't drink any more, so they obviously don't know what they're talking about.

*

Lindy-May asked me for my home phone number. It wasn't a request to step up our friendship, simply that Hilary wants to be able to ring me about the pilot.

*

I happened to drive up Brian and Sheelagh's old street on my way home, today.

The new reiki healer is actually *in* their former home.

*

I wonder how *he* is getting on doing the interview with Mark. He thanked me again this morning for suggesting it and said Mark had only agreed to do it because of our friendship. I hadn't really thought of Mark and myself as friends, yet. The only thing we have in common is our recurring anxiety, and currently even that seems to have lifted.

*

Hilary phoned while I was making the tea, and I immediately went into another hot flush. She wanted to fax me the letter from Hugh, the adopted baby, but I had to explain that I didn't actually have a fax machine in my home. (Surely I'm not alone in this!) I took the opportunity to suggest to her, again, that she needed a professional detective who would have all the right equipment, but she insisted this was not so and I was perfectly placed: Hugh had been born in the town where I now lived. She would e-mail me the contents of his letter tonight.

*

That Millennium Exhibition and Arts Centre flyer is still hanging around, advising me that the word 'hero' is three-quarters made up of 'her'.

*

We had a quick meeting of the Parents' Committee to record the profits of the quiz – more than £500 including the raffle – and to start the preparations for our summer fête. I formally announced that Lindy-May Coulthard and Harry Ferris from Zero FM had agreed to perform the opening ceremony, and those who didn't already know looked suitably impressed. One of the new daddies asked if we thought Harry Ferris would be willing to put his head in the stocks for the wet-sponge-throwing sideshow, which is usually filled by a rota of male teachers. I was relieved when practically everybody reacted negatively, preferring to cherish their minor celebrity broadcaster.

*

When I got home from the meeting, I checked my e-mails dutifully, and there was Hilary's message introducing me to Hugh Davy. According to his letter, Hugh is a thirty-five-year-old bus driver who lives with his wife Jenny and their boy and girl, aged six and four. Hugh has long known he was adopted, but it wasn't until he had his own children that he expressed a wish to know more and discovered he had been a foundling. As his adoptive parents were fit, well and had no objections, he had decided he would try to find out about his biological origins. He wanted to know, for example, if there was any hereditary illness in his background, any special talent. He didn't want to upset anyone who might have moved on, but he felt entitled at least to know who had given him life.

It was a straightforward letter sounding as though it came from a stable, straightforward man, and I could see why Hilary thought she could work with him. She'd tagged on a message of her own, suggesting that a foundling in the town must have been big news thirty-five years ago and that the story might have been covered by our local newspaper. So, if I can get Eleanor to babysit tomorrow afternoon, that's where I'm going to start.

*

He says his interview with Mark went really well. Mark's shop is full of beautiful things and real curiosities, and everything comes with a tale attached, which should make for an interesting article. I told him that Lindy-May had visions of Mark extending the business to include a coffee shop, and *he* was really enthusiastic. He said the steading is faced with cut stone and has exquisite views of the mountains, not a mobile-phone mast in sight, and the village is crying out for somewhere for visitors to take refreshment. But why would Mark go to the bother? Even in the course of the interview, he was interrupted to make a sale of a 1930s art-deco bedroom set at £1,500 and an oak secretaire (which *he* would have loved, had we the money and/or space) for a haggled-down £1,200.

*

Tomorrow night is gourmet night. This sounds as though it should involve oysters or lamb or lots of other things we never eat. We must be the only people who regard beef stew as a delicacy.

* * *

The civil-servant shoplifter has actually written to the Riverside shopping mall manager to complain about me! He has been off on sick leave with stress for the past nine months so he won't be bothering himself about it, but it's bothering me, and it's certainly bothering Ted Twome, although he's assuring me to the contrary. All the girls in the canteen say I shouldn't worry about it and are calling the woman a nutter. Brenda says the same woman comes to her sometimes for extra-long cigarettes and is bizarre even to pass the time of day with. None of this makes me feel much better. I'm still thinking, Why me? I only spoke to her. I'm not even the one who handed her over to the police.

After my shift, I bought the requisite items for my beef and bean casserole, took them home and set off again to begin my investigations at the newspaper. If I'm going to have two jobs, I don't know how I'm going to find time for proper cooking.

*

I bumped into Michelle, my afternoon counterpart, as I came past Shoerama. I felt it only polite to stop and speak to her for once, so I asked how her university access course was going. She said she loves it. She'd been miserable in school – who wasn't? – but she's in with a really good learning group now, and she can't get enough of it. It turns out that her tutor is the same person who takes the 'shero' classes at the Millennium Exhibition and Arts Centre. Michelle has started going there as well. She told me that eighty per cent of the children's books published today feature male heroes and that traditionally women's natural magic has been suppressed by a male priesthood. I didn't know either of those things. Do I have any natural magic? (Not so as you'd notice.)

I also ran into Marilyn Softly, former special-needs co-ordinator at my children's school and my erstwhile employer on her funky ethical market stall, with her friend Miss Morning, our children's retired school principal. They were coming out of Sandwich, Sandwich. Miss Morning was bursting to tell me Marilyn's news, which was that she'd been 'spotted' at an ecology trade fair by an environmentally friendly clothing company, and they had asked her to model for their next catalogue. She'll be showing off their clothes, jewellery and accessories in full colour on unbleached paper. Marilyn was playing it down, but I could tell she was chuffed. She said they won't be paying her supermodel wages or anything, but she's going to do it just for the fun of it.

I asked cautiously how her stall was going, and she said, 'So-so.' She has been doing some market research to help her decide whether it's worthwhile to keep going and has discovered that she would probably get a lot more business if she had the air of permanency created by shop premises instead of a mere marketplace table. But, even in our little town, permanent premises are expensive, so it would be a gamble. Marilyn hasn't yet decided what to do.

*

The newspaper people were very helpful. At least, Veronica, the receptionist, who you get the feeling actually runs the place, was. She explained that the old papers are kept in storage and she would have to send for them, which she would happily do if I provided her with dates. I gave her Hugh Davy's date of birth. I didn't know if the story I was looking for even existed, I explained, but Veronica said it was worth a try. She ordered me a month's newspapers from the weeks immediately after the birth, just to be sure we'd looked properly. She advised me to return on Monday, when they should be waiting for me. I have to read them in the office – I'm not allowed to take them away.

*

Big news at the amalgamated magazine. *His* old editor is leaving and took *him* out to lunch to break it to him. He said he'd spent enough years watching other people get rich as self-starters, and now it was time for him to do it. He has negotiated a small redundancy package, but mostly he's going to make his fortune by becoming a property tycoon in Bulgaria. When you look at some of the half-wits who are making a killing out there, he said, it can't be that difficult. He offered to find us a property and sell it to us for cost price.

As if. We can't even afford to put a coat of paint on the house we have, although our overdraft has stopped growing since I got this job. And what with having access to a cut-price hairdresser as well, I'm feeling comparatively loaded. Which reminds me, I must make another appointment with Janice. I could get used to getting my hair back-washed and professionally dried every week.

But I do feel sorry for *him*. Last year, his womanising best friend, Woods, had a serious heart attack, followed by bypass surgery, and during his recuperation re-fell in love with his 'long-suffering wife', Wendy. They moved away to 'try again'. So far, they seem to have stuck together, but it meant that *he* got left behind, with his editor at *Go For It* the nearest thing he had to a buddy, and now he's leaving, too. I mean, I'd like to think that *he* and I are friends, at last, but it's not the same thing. So I'm truly sorry for him.

* * *

I called in with Janice at my tea break and made another hair appointment for Monday. While I was there, she told me they were thinking of allowing a nail bar to set up within the salon, and she was sounding out her clients. The service would be provided by a self-employed outsider, so the prices would be at a commercial, not subsidised, rate but people could have their nails done while they were under the drier, for example, or waiting for their colours or perms to take hold. If there's enough positive feedback, Moira Reynolds will allow the nail technician to set up for a month's trial.

I didn't know what to say. I don't see the point of having gilded nails when I've such ugly teeth. Pity there's no such thing as a tooth bar.

*

This week's bonny-baby winner is a little blonde angel called Molly. The consensus in the canteen is that she'll be hard to beat. I hope she'll look after her teeth.

*

I rang Hilary and told her I'd set the ball rolling in my search for Hugh's story in the local paper. She was pleased, although I sensed she wished things could move a bit faster.

She asked if I was coming to the Zero FM St Patrick's Night party. I'd known nothing about it. Hilary, who doesn't seem to bother much with tact, said she'd thought perhaps Lindy-May would have invited me. She hadn't.

* * *

Kathleen and Lorna called in to see me this morning with their surrogate grand-offspring. Apparently Fiona and Simon are taking the boys to France for their summer holidays and have asked Lorna and Kathleen to go too, all expenses paid. (This is the first time I've heard anyone use the expression 'all expenses paid' in earnest, in real life. I always thought it was one of those telly expressions that no one ever really said, like 'follow that cab.') They don't know what to do. On the one hand, they said, it's an adventure. On the other, they're afraid there'll be nothing they can eat, and they don't speak the language.

I pointed out that there are probably branches of their new favourite Tasty Ranch throughout France, and all they really need to be able to say is 'hello', 'please' and 'thank you', because they can point at most things. They still looked dubious.

Kathleen's other worry is that the nursing-home will decide that, in the very fortnight they'll be away, Walter is ready to return to his own house, and she'll have to be there to look after him. I said she can't just never go anywhere for the rest of her life on the off-chance that Walter might be released from captivity. I don't know what they'll choose to do.

*

Ted Twome's wife was with him in the canteen at tea-break time. Even if she hadn't been sitting with him, I'd have worked out who she was. She is a shorter, frumpier version of Cheryl the PR girl – an equally pretty if fun-size model of the same thing.

I sat with Moira Reynolds. She didn't mention the civil-servant shoplifter business, just asked how I was managing the job and the children. I said it was working out fine. By the time I'd finished my shift and had my lunch in the canteen, it was time to do my first school lift, and some days, like today, my parents would collect the children to give me a little extra time. (I didn't tell her about my new second job. I thought that information might be better kept to myself.) Moira said she remembered when her daughter was small, and she, Moira, always seemed to be running between work and school with no time to herself, but now Penny was doing her A levels – practically grown up – and it seemed like a blink since she was traipsing out of school in knee socks, her Barbie lunchbox in hand. Children are hard work, but I still don't want mine to grow up too quickly. Penny is taking psychology, chemistry and biology A levels. She wants to go to university and become a forensic psychologist.

*

I enjoyed my back-wash at the hairdresser's so much that I think it's going to be the hot-foam car-wash all over again.

*

The old newspapers have arrived. When I entered the office, Veronica nearly leaped over the counter to greet me. She was so excited. The story I was looking for had been front-page news in the week that little Hugh Davy was born. 'Foundling!' read the headline, with an outline of the story and a signpost to more inside. (I noticed the by-line with interest.) There was a big photograph of a days-old Hugh and the information that he had provisionally been named Noel, because it was nearly Christmas. I read the story from start to finish, twice, and wondered how on earth I was supposed to know which bits of it were clues. I dare say they had a photocopier in the building, but I was too shy to ask to use it, so instead I pulled out the notebook I had bought in the stationer's/wannabe bookshop and tried to write everything down.

The story was: one dark and snowy night (yes, really) in December 1972, a young local woman called Sally Lewis was walking from her marital home at Wellington Park to her place of work, the town's small hotel. Somewhere along the way, she heard the squalling of a catfight, which she didn't bother with. She wasn't much of a cat-lover and was in a hurry to get to work and indoors out of the snow. But when the cries continued to ring in her ears as she strode on through the cold, she'd the unexpected thought that perhaps it was not cats, but some other being that was emitting the noise. It crossed Sally Lewis's mind that it was, in fact, a baby.

A mother, whose own little boy was tucked up in bed at home with his daddy looking after him, she turned on her heel and tried to establish exactly where the sound was coming from. She followed it through the lichgate of the church she'd just passed, up the footpath and to the porch. The door was half closed, and behind it lay a baby, wrapped in old towels and placed in a laundry basket.

Sally ran to the nearest phone box and rang for an ambulance, then hurried back to the lichgate, where she stood shivering to wave the ambulance down and show the crew the way. The baby was taken straight to hospital. There was a large photograph of him in the newspaper and a smaller picture of the outside of the church but no photos of Sally Lewis or the laundry basket.

*

When I got home, Eleanor made me a cup of coffee, which I thought was nice of her, but while I was drinking it she asked me a question which amounted to, had I ever switched on the vacuum cleaner since I'd got this store-detective job? Of course she would ask this on the one day when I'd been swanning about getting my hair done and looking up old newspaper reports. Every other day, I've a packed routine of school pick-ups, washing lunchboxes, making the next day's lunches, preparing our evening meal, homework, music practice, uniform checks, bedtime stories . . . Not for the first time, I want to know how mothers who work full-time make it all happen.

I told Eleanor about the Hugh Davy thing, and she said nothing, but her look told me she thought I should keep away from this one. Is it too late for me to back out? She also said, in a throwaway fashion, that Terry is making noises about returning to poetry-writing – which wasn't a throwaway remark at all. My father hasn't written a poem in twenty years, and it's an open secret in our family that he was half crazy all the years he was writing. From what I now know, I'd say he suffered from chronic anxiety, but that's not a term any of us would dare use. Eleanor always said it would make anyone go a bit doo-lally sitting up there in the attic all the time with only the spiders for company.

*

The time-and-motion person has given everybody at the magazine a time sheet, on which they're supposed to fill in their tasks and what time they started and finished each one. *He's* raging. He says it's an imposition and an insult. But he still has to do it.

* * *

Kathleen, Lorna and the boys were in the mall again this morning, buying a Sudoku magazine and a box of man-size tissues for Walter. Kathleen said she's going to ask at the nursing-home what would happen if they were ready to discharge Walter and she was in France. Good for Kathleen. She's being proactive. Lorna asked me if I knew whether

124

Pharmacity takes passport pictures. So we can see which way she's leaning.

I'm jealous.

*

It was another Bill Worthington mystery last night. A bit boring. Tonight, in the second and concluding part, we will be treated, no doubt, to some obscure back-story in the last five minutes that will explain everything but which no viewer could possibly have guessed. This is the problem with the Bill Worthington mysteries. At least in *Mac* the audience is treated with some respect.

Today, Lorcan Hinds is in the papers again. They're not the sort of thing I'd normally read, but they're left for us in the canteen. If everybody else is flicking through them over their snacks, I tend to do the same. This time, he's been snapped going into a Hollywood A-list party with Robbie Williams. The celebrity gossip reporter says Lorcan Hinds is charming the pants off the US film industry and that it's only a matter of time before he's grabbed for his first leading-man role. If she's right, this is surely the end of *Mac*.

I popped into the hairdresser's to let Janice know my opinion on the nail-bar proposal. (Because of the suffragettes, Nelson Mandela, etc., I always feel morally obliged to exercise my vote when invited, even in building-society elections.) I told Janice I thought it was a good idea to offer the service for a month, as suggested, to discover if there was a market for it. She said that that was what most people were saying, so she'll ask Moira for the OK to proceed. I doubt I'll ever have my nails done, but I'd say plenty will. Lots of girls in the canteen have long painted talons with little diamante studs. How do they do the dishes?

*

I was buying a packet of spearmint tic tacs at the cigarette counter after my shift when I saw the posh girl thief entering the building. Even though I was off-duty and soon due at school, I followed her for a little in the hope of happening upon Michelle, just to see if my high-fiving colleague reacted in any particular way or gave me any sort of sign. Well, we *did* sort of nearly run into Michelle, but I could swear that when she saw us coming – the girl from the posh school in front, and me a little way behind – she walked away rather quickly in the opposite direction. I'm not much of a conspiracy theorist, but there's definitely something strange going on, and I feel as if I'm the only one who doesn't know what it is.

*

I tried phoning Hilary with my foundling news, but I couldn't get hold of her.

* * *

They've installed new rubber matting between the inner and outer automatic doors at the front of the Riverside shopping mall. The smell is intoxicating. I keep sneaking out there to inhale it.

*

I caught two fifteen-year-old boys stealing chart CDs from the Sounds display in the supermarket. The mall sent for the police but will not be pressing charges as this was the boys' first offence. The silly things put themselves through all this for nothing as the items they attempted to steal were empty display cases.

*

I found Kathleen, Lorna and the children in the juice bar, drinking smoothies. The grannies had to dilute Nathan's and Samuel's with mineral water and ensure they used straws because Fiona had heard on Radio 4 that fruit acids strip enamel off young teeth.

Kathleen has spoken to the matron at Walter's nursing-home and has been told to go to France and enjoy herself. They'll definitely keep Walter if Kathleen is away. The pair of them had been into Pharmacity and had their passport pictures taken. Kathleen couldn't look at hers. Lorna resembled a convict.

*

I managed to get hold of Hilary briefly, but it turns out that this week she's in the middle of negotiating her new contract at Zero FM, so she didn't want to talk, even about matters relating to her beloved pilot programme.

* * *

When Terry was writing before, I was young, and we all lived in the flat at the stately home where my mother was curator. He had a huge attic all to himself where he could work in peace. Now that he and my mother share a modest, though comfortable, retirement bungalow, he has nowhere to isolate himself in order to compose. They did have a little beach flatlet, but after my father used it briefly last year to leave my mother, it has been sold. Consequently, over the past couple of days, Eleanor has attempted to vacate her home while my father establishes a new writing habit in the spare bedroom. She has come to our house, which is empty all morning when we are out. Rather than sit around doing nothing or watching Fern Britton, she's spent the time spring-cleaning us. It's fabulous. I mean, she hasn't tackled anything intense, like the encrusted oven, but she's vacuumed and dusted everywhere and has done out the boys' bedrooms. I wonder if I should offer her money.

*

Tanya was in the mall today. My brain recognised her face as familiar and I had smiled and said 'hello' before the information filtered through that she was Mark's ex-girlfriend, whom I had visited at their canal-side apartment. She, in turn, had automatically helloed at me, then stopped and looked puzzled, as if she had no idea who I was. I'm used to this.

I explained reluctantly that I was the person who had come looking for Mark. Tanya said, 'Oh, yes,' and peered at me again, as if I should be familiar but wasn't. She surprised me then by asking if I wanted to go for coffee. I explained in an undertone that I couldn't, I was a store detective.

Tanya's eyes went involuntarily to epauletted Leon, who was hovering over a crowd of kids at the sweet rack in front of the cigarette counter.

I could see what she was thinking. 'They're security,' I explained. 'I'm undercover.'

Now she was thinking that, if it came to a struggle, she'd rather have me to contend with than burly Leon. 'I just spot them,' I went on. 'They stop them leaving the building.'

This seemed to satisfy her. 'Anyhow,' said Tanya. 'You found him.'

I said I had.

Then, as though I didn't know, she told me Mark was staying with Lindy-May and he and she had split up.

To show concern, I asked if she thought the split was permanent. To my surprise – because I thought Mark had made it pretty clear it was over between them – she said she hoped they'd be getting back together. I tried not to look shocked. She admitted that Mark had asked her to move out of the flat within six months, but she thought this had come more from Lindy-May than from Mark and that he'd change his mind when he was properly well again. She said it had been hard not seeing him, first when he was hiding out at Brian and Sheelagh's and then when Lindy-May had taken him in and shut her, Tanya, out. But she'd heard that Mark was back in the shop, and no one could stop her calling on him there. Apparently unburdened, and, I reflected afterwards, having asked nothing about me or my life, she strode off on her long, racehorse legs.

*

I bought Eleanor some flowers in the supermarket. I used my laminated discount card.

*

I couldn't be bothered with gourmet night. We had fish-fingers, peas and Premium Select oven chips, also from the supermarket and actually quite good.

* * *

There is a big hoo-ha in the canteen over this week's results of the bonny-baby competition. According to today's paper, the winner is Jordan Tate, a boy whose looks do not instantly leap off the page as those of a child model. His ears are not only extremely large but sit at an angle of ninety degrees to his head. He has sparse hair, narrow eyes and looks to be grunting rather than smiling at the camera. His sturdy form is almost bursting from the borrowed dungarees. Of course, I understand that, to his parents, he's a thing of beauty, but the shop-girls were unanimously convinced that this week's winner should be Macy Jones, a sweet little girl with coffee-coloured skin and sapphire-blue eyes. Outraged, they are demanding a recount.

Moira Reynolds and I tried to point out that the format

of the competition means the child with the most votes wins, regardless of beauty, and the girls have now decided that the whole thing is therefore nonsense, as any parent can buy their way to the final by submitting enough voting slips. Well, that was always the case. (The final will be judged by an impartial panel, including a representative of the Riverside shopping mall, the editor of the local newspaper, the photographer who took the pictures and, possibly, someone from Zero FM.) The great thing for sales of the newspaper is that no parent knows how many voting slips will be enough. Should they buy fifty papers? A hundred? A hundred and fifty?

*

I saw a young, scrawny man steal a bale of nappies from Nursery World today. I let him go. Am I becoming a maverick? A law unto myself? Am I 'When good store detectives go bad . . .?'

*

I've been trying to put off thinking about it until I can speak to Hilary, but I can't help wondering how on earth we're going to begin to track down whoever left Baby Noel (now Hugh Davy) in the laundry basket at the church in 1972. We have no name, no age, no address and nothing in the way of a description. In other words, we have virtually nothing to go on. Unless she's bursting to be found, I don't see what chance we have. I don't know how much of this story Hugh is aware of, or how much it may dash his hopes. I also want to mention the by-line to Hilary.

*

This evening, I dropped Eleanor home from our house. She'd walked up this morning, but the weather had changed. I popped my head round the door to speak to Terry. He was full of chat. At about a hundred miles an hour. That's the nature of the illness, I suggest. Give him a few weeks like this and he'll crash and burn. I hope the poems are worth it.

*

He has done a complete turnaround and fallen in love with his time sheet. He says he didn't realise until he saw it all written down just how much he does in the course of a day or a week. Naturally, he would love to get a look at horrible Jeremy's, but he doesn't think his own is too shabby. He was so pleased that he took us to the Tasty Ranch for tea. The children had Tasty Young 'Uns, and we had Sheriff T. Steakburgers. Things are looking up.

* * *

The forsythia is in bloom. I cannot say this even inside my own head without the words assuming the voice of Celia Johnson in *Brief Encounter*. 'The forsythia is in bloom.' It really is.

*

Do I need to advise Mark that Tanya is harbouring expectations of reconciliation – or mind my own business? Probably the latter. When I stop to think about it, how well do I actually know Mark? Perhaps he and Tanya break up and get back together all the time. I'd better keep my nose out.

*

I've broached the subject of the Easter holidays with the children. I wondered if they'd enjoy attending the council-run play scheme at the leisure centre for two weeks. They could go there on a mornings-only basis, and I could still look after them in the afternoons.

Well, the weeping and gnashing of teeth was unbelievable. Much worse than last year when their father fell in love with my Listening Angel befriender and trainee reiki healer Prentiss Prine and left us for her and her dog, Earl. Our eldest son said that if I make him go to the play scheme he'll kill himself. Not that he's trying to be manipulative or anything. I really don't feel I can foist them on Eleanor. She has enough on her plate with my father just now.

*

Horrible Jeremy bought cakes and pastries for everyone in the office at morning tea break to ward off the Monday blues. *He* is seething. And wondering how to compete. I suggested I could pick him up a couple of apple tarts from the home bakery after work. He'll think about it.

*

No crime drama tonight. Instead, there was a programme where they got celebrities to do horse- and cat-whispering. The celebrities are going to work on this all week, and we, the viewers, are going to be shown the highlights of their efforts every night. First time out, Malandra Burrows was the best. Clive Anderson couldn't do it at all, plus his horse stood on his foot. Why do I watch this crap? Interestingly, there was no hint of dog-whispering. Perhaps dog-lovers are inclined to be more traditional in their methods.

* * *

Shouting Barbara has rumbled me. It has only taken her two months, but she's finally noticed that I'm present in the Riverside mall as often as she is − i.e., every day. This morning she shouted at me from the supermarket café: 'HERE! DO YOU WORK HERE? DO YOU WORK IN THIS PLACE?' My conscience told me it was fundamentally wrong to mislead such an *ingénue*, but a more desperate imperative told me I'd promised myself I'd pay for a holiday and a built-in wardrobe in the back bedroom before my time at the mall was finished, and the more desperate impulse won. I claimed I didn't work in the mall but merely, like her, visited often. I swung my empty shopping-bag and handbag, as if to prove the point. I reminded Barbara that I had used to work in the Listening Angels charity shop off the high street, and that she'd been a frequent visitor there, too. Although there was no sign that she remembered me from there, this seemed to do the trick. She asked, 'DO YOU KNOW KATHLEEN?' To which I was glad to reply, honestly, that I did. And Lorna. And, as if specifically to corroborate my story, who then appeared but Kathleen,

Lorna and the double buggy. They acknowledged Barbara, who went back to her cooked breakfast and her complimentary *Daily Mirror*, and told me they were off to Pharmacity again as Fiona and Simon had asked them to get the boys' passport photos taken, too.

Half an hour later, I saw Kathleen and Lorna once more, this time haggard and careworn. They had had a nightmare time trying to get the photos done. They simply couldn't convey to Nathan and Samuel the concept of *not* smiling for their pictures. Every time the Pharmacity woman raised the camera in front of either of them, they lit up like Christmas trees. What began as sweetly funny soon descended into frustration and, after numerous failed attempts, the grannies became desperate and briefly lost their minds: they told the boys that if they didn't stop smiling, Kathleen and Lorna would have to leave them in Pharmacity with the camera woman and go home without them. Naturally, the boys went berserk. Kathleen and Lorna tried to backtrack and say they hadn't meant it, but the children were howling too hysterically to hear. The grannies tried putting them back into the double buggy to remove them from the scene of the trouble, but the boys' little backs and limbs were rigid with distress so Kathleen and Lorna couldn't bend them into a sitting-in-buggy shape. Eventually, they each lifted one stiff child and carried him out of Pharmacity while the assistant gladly wheeled out the empty buggy. They managed to lug the wailing children to the sweet rack in front of the supermarket cigarette counter and let them choose a soothing treat. This was a difficult decision for the grannies to take as it flew in the face of Fiona and Simon's Absolutely No Sweets directive, but they were desperate.

They're going to confess all to Fiona and Simon because they don't want them finding out from the boys. But they're afraid they'll have spoiled everything, now, and they'll get the sack and not be invited to France. Privately, I thought they should have told the boys that the treats were called 'salad' and then the children could have said what they wanted and the parents would have been none the wiser. But really, the grannies are right. Honesty is the best policy. Barbara's on my conscience.

*

The April issue of *Go For It* magazine, incorporating *Self-Starters' Monthly* came out today. Mark Strain is on the front cover.

* * *

Lindy-May is having a party at her house on Easter Monday. She has invited us to bring the children. She also wants me to ask Eleanor and Terry, as Mark is keen to meet Terry, being an erstwhile fan of his poetry. I said I'd pass on the invitation. To tell the truth, I'm reluctant. I've only just acquired Mark's friendship, and I don't want him to become more Terry's friend than mine.

*

Hilary finally returned my calls. She's delighted to hear that I've tracked down the local newspaper's coverage of the baby story and that they gave it such a splash. I summarised what it said, and, like me, she was disappointed that there were no real clues to the mother's identity, but when I told her that the by-line was none other than Sandy Long's, she whistled and said it would be worth talking to him 'when he gets back' in case he remembered anything significant he had found out at the time but had been unable to print.

When he gets back? It turns out that Sandy Long is currently in Australia recording a special series on expatriates and that when he's finished it, he'll stay Down Under for a couple of weeks' holiday. He won't be around for about a month. Still, Hilary says she's glad we've made a start, and she'll bring Hugh Davy up to speed.

*

I prevented a crime today. I saw a man put a pocket guidebook into his pocket in the stationer's/wannabe bookshop. Seeing Tony nearby, I scooted over and told him. He went and stood behind the man, who went red and put the book back on the shelf. Maybe he was just trying it for size, to see if it really was a *pocket* guide.

* * *

Our staff training session this morning was about diabetes (why?) and comprised a talk by the surprisingly entertaining specialist diabetes nurse from the hospital, culminating in finger-prick testing for all of us by a team of student nurses. Two people came up positive and now have to see their GPs: Brenda from the cigarette counter and the heavy woman from the discount jeweller's.

*

Michelle, my afternoon counterpart, was in the canteen when I was having lunch (Spanish omelette, 90p). She's on 'Easter vacation' from her university access course at the further-education college and had popped in to make a hair appointment with Janice.

Michelle wants to do a qualification in social work, and her access course includes modules in sociology, psychology and English. Her current module is English, and her current text is *The Great Gatsby*. I loved it when I read it. I asked Michelle, quoting a rather obvious exam-type question, 'So, is Gatsby really "great"?' I was remembering the Dionysian revelry at his mansion and his big golden car – I was thinking of the symbolism. Michelle said 'yes', as in 'yes, you idiot, it's in the title.' I backed off.

*

Eleanor has warned me that if I don't start wiping the kitchen surfaces, sweeping the floor and emptying the rubbish a bit more often, we will get mice. I'm terrified of this prospect. I'm terrified of mice. However, I don't follow the logic of her argument: surely a mouse or mice would have to have made its/their way into our house in order to discover the ready supply of crumbs and food scraps. In which case, we would already have a mouse/mice, wouldn't we?

Eleanor has solved the Easter childcare crisis: she'll come up to our house and look after the children. She says she's not welcome in her own bungalow while Terry's writing – the slightest noise seems to break his concentration – so, providing I'm home by lunchtime, it suits her perfectly. Terry's new morning blueprint is to stay in bed with a flask of tea and a beanbag lap tray and do his writing there. He quits for the day at eleven, at which time he takes a shower. When he's working, routine is everything.

*

I told Eleanor about the party invitation to Lindy-May's on Easter Monday. She looked uncertain, which is unusual for her. She said she'd talk it over with Terry. I hope she doesn't think she's doing me any favours – I'd be quite happy if they stayed away.

* * *

Phew. Order has been restored in the universe. The 'right' child won this week's heat of the bonny-baby competition. His name is Vishnu Nash, and the canteen girls agree he has the longest, thickest, sootiest eyelashes you've ever seen. Who knew there were so many such beautiful children in this little town?

* * *

Moira has told me I'm entitled to two days' holiday for Easter, and I can either take them now or save them up and take them later, in lieu. If I take them now, I can either have Friday and Monday or Monday and Tuesday. I said I'd take Monday and Tuesday. That's Monday to get ready for Lindy-May's party and Tuesday to recover. (As if I need to recover from my standard glass and a half of red wine spread over the duration, or none at all if it's my turn to drive.)

*

Mark Strain came into the mall this morning. He needed some stamps and couldn't find any at Lindy-May's. He invited me to have a cuppa with him at the gourmet coffee place. I explained that I couldn't sit down with him because I was on duty, but I could loiter by his table for a chat. We decided to do that. Mark drinks espresso. (Yuk.)

Brian and Sheelagh, who are retired, are going to mind his shop later this week as he has to go to two auctions to buy more stock. They've done this before and quite enjoy it, and Mark trusts them. I asked if he knew that a new reiki healer had opened up in their old house, and he said, yes, someone had told him. He asked me if I'd ever had a reiki treatment, and I said that I had, but only by a trainee, not a master, so I might not have got the full effect. Mark said that he wasn't particularly drawn to New Age stuff but that he might give it a try.

He was less convinced about the cuddle parties. I didn't know what they were. He said that, as well as hosting reiki healing, Brian and Sheelagh's old house is the venue for cuddle parties, where strangers come together to meet their need to touch and be touched. There's nothing rude about it. It's above board and properly organised. I tried to imagine it and didn't like what I saw. Surely such meetings would be attended by all those people with body odour, halitosis, facial warts or beards who couldn't get a hug any other way. I didn't say this in case Mark thought I was shallow. Instead, I dropped into the conversation that I had been speaking to Tanya. Mark said, 'Oh,' but neither of us picked up the baton.

I noticed that he was wearing his leather jacket with his left arm in its sleeve and the right sleeve slung over his right shoulder, as if that arm were injured and in a sling, but his right arm seemed to be working fine.

*

Hilary phoned tonight (and made me miss the new crime drama about a mysterious woman with implausibly stiff, shiny hair arriving in a new town, so perhaps I didn't miss much). She started off saying that, on the basis of what was in the newspaper article about Baby Noel, we should try to speak to the clergyman at the church where he was left that dark, snowy night. However, as we discussed it, she formed the impression that this would entail dealing with a bunch of conservative elderly – if not dead – men, and she went off the idea. Then she thought we should start with Sally Lewis, who probably would be alive and might give us our first lead. We agreed to sleep on it.

* * *

Michelle was in the canteen again at lunchtime – she'd just had a cut and colour next door with Janice. She was having the Spanish meatballs (£1.50), like me. I asked her whether she enjoys the strange little job we do, and she said she liked it well enough but she felt a bit isolated and would prefer to be properly part of a team. I said I knew what she meant. I thought about trading on our solidarity as the two 'outsiders' to ask her why nobody wants to confront the posh girl, but something stopped me because I just don't know Michelle at all well. If I raise this matter with anyone, it had better be someone who isn't in any way complicit, like Ted Twome or Moira Reynolds.

I don't know what the dress code is for Lindy-May's party, and she hasn't been in the canteen this week to ask.

* * *

This morning, I nabbed another shoplifter in the super-market, but I'm suspicious of my motive in pursuing her. My original reason was that she'd bought her baby-in-a-buggy a hard lolly – the kind like a round boiled sweet on a stick. I never buy those for my children, who are much older, in case the sweet pops off the stick and chokes them. If, by misfortune, they manage to get their hands on one, I make them sit up straight on the sofa and not jump about until they've finished it. So, it was my prejudice against people who give these things to small children that made me follow the woman, and nothing else. Then, when she started to steal, she stole exclusively for herself: a big pair of summer shorts, a beach kaftan and a pair of sunglasses, which she put into her capacious shoulder bag. She took nothing for her child. This struck me as selfish. When she attempted to leave the supermarket, I gave the nod to Leon. We stopped her and went through the usual procedure – but I can't help wondering, am I power-crazed? Is this job teaching me to play God?

*

Hilary phoned again last night and said she thought we should definitely proceed down the Sally Lewis path. I've been charged with going through the local telephone directory to find her, then setting up a rendezvous. Part of me hopes she won't be in the phone book. A large part. Hilary also passed on a message from Lindy-May about her Easter Monday party. She said to come for six o'clock and to bring Kathleen and Lorna as well as Eleanor and Terry. The more the merrier. I see what's going to happen here. All my friends and family are going to make friends with all my other friends, and then none of them will need me.

*

I bought *him* a couple of boxes of instant cappuccino sachets. I thought they might go down well as a treat at the office.

*

Running my finger down the page of Lewises, I hoped I wouldn't find any in our town. But there it was: Lewis, S., 29

Wellington Park. They hadn't even moved house in the thirty-five years since it had happened. I put off ringing until the children were in bed, trying to buy time, but Hilary would undoubtedly call again for a progress report, so I couldn't procrastinate for ever. So I rang, hoping with every trill that the Lewises wouldn't pick up, that they'd be out.

No such luck. A woman answered the phone. I asked for Mrs Lewis. It was her. There was nothing for it but to swallow my nerves, introduce myself and explain my mission. Who knew? Maybe she'd be delighted to hear of Baby Noel again. Perhaps she was continually wondering what had become of him, the little mite she'd found in a snowy porch, cradled in a laundry basket.

Nope. Sally Lewis was *not* pleased to hear why I was calling, she was *not* pleased to hear that Baby Noel was looking for his birth mother, and she would *not* like to meet up to chat about what had happened that dark, snowy night in 1972. She was looking after all three of her grandchildren, who were off school and nursery for the Easter break, and she was trying to get them settled. It had not helped her cause one bit that I had made the phone ring. I said I was sorry, but, with a tenacity I didn't feel, I urged her not to turn me down without thinking about it and asked her to name a more convenient time for me to call her tomorrow.

With reluctance in her voice, and the clear desire to get me off the phone, she said I could ring her at eleven o'clock. I said I would.

What am I going to do? I can't ring her at eleven o'clock tomorrow – I'll be in work. And Hilary can't ring her – Lindy-May will be on the air. I've fucked up.

* * *

This morning's staff training was on healthy eating. A woman told us about food labelling, how to read it and how you have to be careful when comparing products because some are labelled per item and some per hundred grams, and it's up to you to make sure you're comparing like with like. She threw out a few questions to see what we knew, and it turned out that Cheryl, our PR girl, knew more than anybody about food labelling, and possibly more than the woman herself, because she was able to tell us that low-fat yogurts aren't always all they're cracked up to be because they're still full of sugar, and she means *full* of sugar, sometimes twenty grams per pot. The only ones worth bothering with are Weightwatchers' because they're low in fat *and* sugar. I noticed that Ted Twome was looking at Cheryl with something like pride. I also noticed that Cheryl is one of those completely unfairly constructed women who get to have a small bottom and a large chest.

*

Kathleen and Lorna were in the mall today, and I managed to speak to them briefly. They had got over their trauma with the boys' passport photographs and told all to Fiona and Simon who, while not thrilled that their vulnerable children had been threatened with abandonment, nevertheless agreed that anyone can have a bad day/make a mistake, etc., and that they were lucky to have two such devoted 'grannies' as Kathleen and Lorna. Too bloody true. So, they're still on course for France, and the grannies had come into the mall to look for sleeveless blouses and possibly sandals.

I told them they were invited to Lindy-May's Easter Monday party. Well, they puffed up so much they looked fit to burst. We discussed how they'd get there. Our car would be full. Eleanor and Terry would have room in theirs, but they hadn't said definitely they were going, and I don't make transactions on behalf of other people. It was agreed that the best plan was a minicab. I told them I'd call them when I got home to give them Lindy-May's phone number so they could ring her and tell her themselves that they were coming. I haven't seen her in the canteen all week, I don't know why.

I notice that Lorna has started to call Kathleen 'Kate'. What's that about? And is this exclusive to Lorna, or are we all meant to join in?

*

With special permission from Moira Reynolds, I took my break at ten fifty-five and nipped out to the phone booth to call Sally Lewis. Her mood was no better. She was still trying to look after her three grandchildren. We couldn't come to see her during the school holidays – it would be impossible with the youngsters around. If we'd wait until she had them off her hands, she'd see what she could do. I think she said she was 'bad with her nerves'. I said all right and thanked her. At least I could tell Hilary I'd spoken to her.

*

I had salad and a cup of tea for lunch (£1.10). The coleslaw was a bit too oniony.

*

Does spaghetti Bolognese count as gourmet food? Maybe if I put a glass of red wine in it.

* * *

The girls in the canteen couldn't agree on a clear natural winner in the final week of the bonny-baby competition, but no one argued about the readers' votes, which elected Julia Thomas, a little waif-like blonde thing with tattered-looking hair. The judging panel is meeting here, tonight, in the canteen, to decide first, second and third places.

Our photo from the quiz night made it into the paper at last. Lindy-May is very photogenic. Harry Ferris looks his age but appears full of mischief. Caroline, our secretary, looks kind, as always.

* * *

A postcard has come from Marilyn Softly in Cornwall, where she's currently on a photo-shoot for the ethical trading catalogue. She says the skies and the sea are utterly blue in the spring sunshine but that the wind off the water would slice you in two as you stand there modelling tea-dresses and hippie tops, trying not to go purple with cold. She says she could weep for the poor girls who are modelling the unbleached cotton-jersey underwear.

*

I went along to the announcement of the bonny-baby competition winners. Ted Twome was there, on a little stage kept in the storeroom for such occasions. There were large photos of the five contenders attached to a screen behind him. Cheryl was standing in the first row in front of the stage, looking attentive in a coral wrap-over top and a tight pencil skirt. I looked for Nathan and Samuel in their buggy, or any sign of Kathleen and Lorna, but I couldn't see them in what was quite a crowd.

Cheryl had hired face-painters and a balloon modeller to keep the children occupied, and every now and then I heard the bang of another balloon being burst. Ted did a lot of talking into the ear of the photographer, and then in the ear of a man I took to be the editor of the local paper, and then into the ear of Jane Dare, the late-night presenter from Zero FM, who wore a pair of sunglasses and looked as though she hadn't been to bed yet.

Eventually, Ted approached the microphone, welcomed the hordes and said that, without further ado, he would announce the winners in reverse order. Julia Thomas, the waif-like child, came third, winning a £200 shopping voucher and a framed print of her bonny-baby photo. Vishnu Nash came second and received a £300 voucher plus print. I held my breath for Nathan, but first place went to Molly, the blonde-ringleted one who had been the favourite of the canteen. Nathan had the ignominy of being unplaced, like rough-looking Jordan Tate. Ted Twome asked the crowd to give a big cheer for the winners and got a limp roar. Cheryl started determinedly to clap, and there was almost-but-not-quite a round of applause. Then the swarm round the stage began to disperse. I went off to look in the clothes shops for something to wear at Lindy-May's Easter Monday party.

* * *

Just as I feared they would, Mark Strain and Terry, my father, got on like a house on fire. Mark actually brought two books of my father's poems to the party and sheepishly asked Terry to sign them, which he, equally embarrassed, did. Lindy-May came over to see what was going on, and although she isn't a poetry-lover, even she knew 'Girl on a Gate' and asked Terry to read/recite it, which, of course, he declined to do.

As usual, I found it difficult to mix. How do other people do it? I talked to Hilary for a bit because we had business to discuss – the hunt for Hugh Davy's mother – but I'm not great on small talk, so I went outside and watched the children playing with the dogs. As I was the designated driver, *he* had a wonderful time drinking gin and tonic in the conservatory with Harry and Lindy-May, laughing and roaring increasingly as the evening wore on. A few times I went past the window, trying to look purposeful but succeeding only in looking prim in my sobriety.

Eleanor seemed to fall in particularly with Brian and Sheelagh, who were also there and are of similar vintage. They have living-in-retirement-bungalows in common too. I sat beside them for a little while and listened to Sheelagh telling Eleanor the benefits of a new kind of vacuum cleaner you can get fitted into the walls of your house so that you need only attach a hose. Eleanor then told Sheelagh about the benefits of the walking club she's joined.

Kathleen and Lorna seemed to have no problem talking to everybody, and I saw that they, like Eleanor, were also part of a secret society of people who knew they were supposed to bring a dessert. (Kathleen and Lorna brought a Bailey's Irish Cream cheesecake, and Eleanor brought two big strawberry meringues.) *He* had carried in the bottle of good red wine (from both of us!) so that I was seen to arrive empty-handed.

The children kept up their dog training in the dark, and I thought the night would never end. When we eventually headed for home, I had to stop the car about two miles down the road so that *he* could get out and vomit in a hedge.

Nobody passed any remarks on my new coral wrap-over top.

* * *

I spent my second day off cleaning the kitchen – I've been considering what Eleanor said about mice. While wiping, sweeping and scrubbing, I also resolved to deal with the posh girl thief. On my return to work, I'll speak to Moira about it. How do I explain my colleagues' distinct lack of co-operation confronting her without landing them right in it? I'll have to think about that.

*

He looked dreadful this morning, after yesterday's indulgence, but he wouldn't hear of taking the day off work. He's too scared that Jeremy will steal a march. Jeremy's profile of the blacksmith is going into the magazine this month, and *he* wants to find something to trump it, to keep it off the front page.

*

I snuck off from cleaning for an hour and a half and watched the crime drama I'd taped last night when we were out. Not very satisfactory. It dabbled in the supernatural, which I tend to find a bit of a cop-out.

* * *

My hot flushes have disappeared, and *he* has come up with a rather plausible theory to explain them. He has pointed out that they tended to occur in the kitchen, with the cooker and the boiler on full blast, while I was making the evening meal *and wearing a polo-neck jumper*. Since I moved out of polo-necks for the spring and the boiler has been turned off until night-time, the hot-flush phenomenon has disappeared. Perhaps it was not a hormonal surge but heat that was causing the symptom.

However, heat neither explains nor excuses the arrival of

facial hair in my life. I'm dismayed to notice, these days, that I've blonde walrus whiskers above my top lip at the corners of my mouth. How long have they been there? And how do I decide when it's sufficiently embarrassing to resort to waxing or electrolysis? (I don't want to be able to twiddle the ends, like Hercule Poirot!) I might pop in and ask Janice the hairdresser – she's the only beauty professional I know.

*

I saw a familiar and unwelcome face at the grabber machines today: the civil-servant shoplifter. She was wearing the green boots she'd had on the day I caught her, but with a patterned skirt and a retro-ish twin set. I hadn't considered the possibility of our culprits coming back to visit, and the sight of her made my heart thump uncomfortably fast in my chest. She looked extremely angry with the machine. Any of us who work there could have told her not to waste her money because nobody ever wins anything, but we're not allowed to do that. And, anyway, I wouldn't have dared approach her. Even from quite a distance, she looks prickly. Instead, I watched her walk away with her cowboy swagger to look in the window of the discount jeweller's. I ducked into Shoerama and did some controlled breathing. I admit I deliberately avoided her.

*

I consulted *him* about the posh girl shoplifter and whether or not I should speak to Ted Twome or Moira Reynolds about what's going on. He said that, on the one hand, it isn't my responsibility to protect my colleagues if they're doing something dishonest, but, on the other, I still have to work with them for another ten weeks.

After due consideration, I've decided just to 'haunt' her if she comes in again, to let her see I'm watching her. She may decide not to call my bluff.

*

I was talking to Michelle, my high-fiving afternoon counterpart, in the canteen this morning. She'd just been in with Janice getting her hair chopped really short and dyed really red. She said she'd done this because of what was happening at her shero classes at the arts centre. She's loving them. The new reiki healer from Brian and Sheelagh's old house is also in the shero group, and she's offered them discounts on their first reiki session if they go to her.

Having had my own bad experience of a reiki healer (trainee), I said nothing about this but instead asked Michelle what she knew about the cuddle parties supposedly being held there. Not only does she know about them but she's going to one later this month. She said a few from the shero class had decided to go. Everybody has to wear pyjamas, apparently, and it's strictly supervised to keep sexual contact out of the equation, and you don't have to hug anybody you don't like. I couldn't go. I know I'd be the person in the room that no one would be willing to cuddle. Still no sign of Lindy-May in the canteen. Perhaps she's away.

* * *

Moira Reynolds has been on a refresher course in health and safety, so that was our topic this morning at staff training. She gave us a little talk, then handed round A4 photocopies of a cartoon scene of a shop floor, and we had to take our pens and put a ring round everything that was a health and safety risk. There were things like a spill on the floor, a shop assistant wearing stiletto heels, a stockroom worker marching along with a pile of boxes so high he couldn't see where he was going, another assistant up a stepladder to fix an overhead display but with no one holding the ladder . . . There were lots. It was probably useful.

At the end of our session, we had another little activity: we lined up to get our annual staff photo done. I've seen the one hanging in the canteen but didn't know it was replaced yearly. I wondered whether I was supposed to be in it, what with being undercover and all, but Moira said the picture would only be seen by staff and trusted visitors and that, yes, I must line up with the others. When the photographer came to arranging us, I had to be moved as I had, unfortunately, stood right in front of Cheryl, and we both happened to be wearing our identical coral wrap-over tops. This was bad for my self-esteem as Cheryl filled her top so, well, fully, while mine hung on me rather limply. The photographer joked about a bit to put us at our ease, but I kept my smile firmly sealed over my ugly teeth. Then, as he was taking the shot, who should pop into the room but Mrs Ted Twome.

Involuntarily, I turned to check that Cheryl and Ted were not standing beside one another – they weren't – and the photographer swore. I was mightily embarrassed. Because of me, the picture had to be taken again.

Kathleen and Lorna were among those caught out by our later Thursday-morning opening. They had been forced to sit on the seats by the grabber machines since just after nine.

Lorna had learned from Walter to call Kathleen 'Kate'. He has been doing it for a lifetime. I don't think I can make the change. Once I've got a name for someone, I find it difficult to alter. Even our children can call Lindy-May 'Lin', but I just can't. I wonder where she is, though. Has she perhaps decided to drop the Riverside mall community? Has she found another, better, staff canteen?

Kathleen and Lorna were in the mall to find a swimsuit for Lorna. She hasn't been swimming for years but says she used to be quite strong in the water and would like to be able to go into the sea with the boys in France. Won't she get her hearing-aid wet? Kathleen didn't think the mall was the best place to look for Lorna's swimsuit. She thinks the supermarket and the discount designer place will only have stringy bikinis for young girls and not the bust-supportive costume Lorna needs.

They also told me that the bonny-baby competition has cost Fiona and Simon a fortune. Because Nathan was a finalist, he received a print of his photograph in a large gold frame, and now, so they aren't treating their children differently, Fiona and Simon are having to fork out for the same size print and frame of Samuel, who didn't do so well in the voting. Of course, Kathleen and Lorna feel terrible because it was they who entered the boys in the competition. Being a Happy Granny sounds like hard work.

*

Janice the hairdresser was in tears in the canteen. Seemingly, Moira has told her she can no longer wear her slippers in the salon as they constitute a health and safety violation.

* * *

Friday the thirteenth always gives me the jitters. I don't know why: I am, after all, a pragmatist and generally not given to supernatural fantasies. The situation was exacerbated today because I'm already stressed due to Eleanor's suggestion about mice. I've been keeping the kitchen immaculate, wiping down the benches and brushing up crumbs, and I've emptied the bin every day before I go to work and every night before I go to bed. But I still find I'm a little too nervous in my own home, and, in bed, I lie in the dark expecting to hear scratching in the attic.

At the weekend, I intend to lift and clear the large and small piles of detritus which have accumulated throughout the house and which have taken on the look of mouse havens. I'll be anxious doing this and will lift everything jumpily and with the tips of my fingers. I had been half hoping Eleanor might do it for me as she's been here all week with the children, but she's had enough to do looking after them without starting on my housework, I suppose. Perhaps if Terry's still writing at the weekend she will come over and help me then.

Also, I telephoned Mark Strain last night, and he said Lindy-May hasn't been away. He didn't suggest any alternative reason why she's gone AWOL from our canteen, and, because I'm slightly paranoid, and probably a bit self-obsessed, I deduce that I am being avoided.

Terry, my father, is unafraid of mice and rats, as far as I know, but fearful of many other things, so it seems I've inherited his anxiety gene but apply it to my own chosen stuff.

*

Today, we had more of a heist than a shoplift in work. A hooded man ran out of Diggers Discount Jewellery with a bundle of gold chains. The staff pressed their alarm, and a huge noise like a siren filled the mall, alerting Tony and Leon. Leon was at the front end of the walkway, but there are *two* sets of double doors, and the nimble runner sent Leon the wrong way and streaked past him through the other doors, which were already open to let a young mother and her toddler through.

Tony and Leon chased the thief out into the car park but couldn't catch him. I was glad they didn't. Not because I wanted him to get away but because he was of a different kind from the relatively amiable thieves we usually encounter, and I feared he might have a knife. Once again, I found my heart racing and had to do my breathing exercises.

*

This afternoon, Lindy-May returned to our canteen. She hardly spoke to me. She just sat there with her instant cappuccino, flipping through the tabloids. I ate my fisherman's pie (£1.10) and tried to do the same.

* * *

The schools are back. Our youngest child says that for tomorrow's News Day he's going to talk about training Lindy-May's dog to take a biscuit from his hand after being made to wait. He's actually going to say, 'My mummy's friend's dog,' which I appreciate, as I'm not exactly inundated with friends, but it troubles me a little because it reminds me that Lindy-May isn't behaving like a friend just now.

It occurred to me over the weekend that she has had us over to her place twice, and I've yet to reciprocate. Could this be the source of the problem? Have I enjoyed her hospitality too freely, and to the tune of five of us, while offering nothing in return? I'd thought we did our socialising at her place because she'd the space and the help and it was easier all round. Perhaps I got it wrong. Perhaps I should invite Lindy-May, Harry, Hilary and Mark home and make them a meal. I'm panicked at the very thought of it.

The schools going back also means it's time to phone Sally Lewis again, and I don't want to. But I must.

*

Janice was in the canteen today, wearing shoes. She says she feels really uncomfortable in them, compared to her slippers, and she's thinking of getting a pair of those air-cushioned trainers to see if that's any better, but she won't be able to wear skirts. As Janice generally wears tracksuit bottoms and a polo shirt, this doesn't strike me as a big problem, but perhaps she dresses differently in summer. I recommended my neighbour Jill's new inset shop within Trevor's old-fashioned emporium as it has some beautiful shoes and now does trainers as well. Then everybody started talking up Jill's place, saying how wonderful it was and mentioning the luxury of her leather sofa in the fitting area. I felt like a good neighbour for starting a bit of a publicity wagon rolling for her.

*

When I phoned Sally Lewis, I got the feeling she'd been waiting for my call, and possibly dreading it. She didn't sound happy to hear from me. I explained about the radio programme and how it was going to follow Hugh Davy's journey to find his birth mother. Sally Lewis recommended we go no further. She urged me to axe the programme – as if I could – because it would do nobody any good. Her hostility made me wonder what she knew that she wasn't telling. Was the baby's mother really a mere unknown stranger or perhaps someone Sally had chosen to protect and was still protecting? I'm not a pushy person, but Hilary had held out the carrot of a possible permanent job, and I have only a little more than two months left of my Riverside mall contract. I urged her at least to meet Hugh Davy. Eventually, she agreed to see him but refused to have any recording made of their conversation. That was the best I could get, but I don't know that Hilary will be overly impressed.

*

There is a new drama tonight from the pen of one of the *Mac* writers. I intend to put my feet up with that, stop worrying about the potential mice and/or Hilary and/or Lindy-May. I've also taken the soothing measure of buying myself a bar of Fry's Chocolate Cream.

* * *

I'm so tired. I could *not* get to sleep last night. I think it was the caffeine in the Fry's Chocolate Cream. I'm a strictly decaffeinated person these days, and I must have become sensitive. I spent the night tossing and turning and trying not to listen for mice. This morning, even Shouting Barbara could see I was ravaged. She yelled at me from the supermarket café: 'HELLO! HELLO! YOU DON'T LOOK A BIT WELL. ARE YOU NOT FEELING WELL?' I admitted that I had felt better, and Barbara advised me to GO AND GET A CUP OF TEA, as this was what she did when she wasn't feeling well. But it wasn't my tea-break time, so I struggled on.

On the plus side, last night's suspense drama was excellent – a cast of unknown actors, and viewer-sympathy was passed round among them so you couldn't see clearly who was a goodie and who a bit dark. It concludes tonight. Kathleen, Lorna and the boys were in, shopping for Walter's birthday. There's not much you can buy for a man who lives in a nursing-home, so Kathleen thought she'd try to get him some nice new pyjamas. It's a bit boring, but I think she knows that, so I didn't say anything. She found him a black pair in the supermarket, which she thought were a bit more glamorous than his usual stripy ones, and she can change them if they don't fit. Lorna bought him a Terry's Chocolate Orange and a bumper puzzle magazine. They got their cards and wrapping paper in the stationer's/wannabe bookshop, and they even got a card from the boys, which Nathan is to write as Fiona and Simon have decided he is to learn to write now and not wait until he's at school. (I think this is a big mistake as he will be bored in class and turn to delinquency. But perhaps I'm just jealous of their having such an advanced, not-to-mention-good-looking, child.)

*

There was a little flurry of excitement in the mall when Molly and her mother, winners of the bonny-baby competition, came in to start spending their £1,000 voucher. Word filtered back to Ted Twome, who came down to greet them as VIPs. Then the mother took Molly to Diggers Discount Jewellery, where she had her baby's ears pierced. I hung about nearby, guiltily fascinated, but I can swear that the child never made a sound. I don't think she even knew they'd been done.

Mother and daughter then went to Nursery World, where they loaded up with new clothes for Molly, and on to the supermarket where they did a big shop. I don't know if they used vouchers or just ordinary money in the supermarket. I don't suppose there was any rule that said the prize had to be used exclusively for Molly's benefit. And, as she presumably already has a cot and a buggy at home, it would be pretty difficult to spend £1,000 all at once in Nursery World, unless the voucher is valid for several years, which I doubt.

*

I was so glad to reach the end of my shift so that I could look forward to getting to bed.

* * *

I'm not having much luck. With fifteen minutes and all of the denouement still to come in last night's concluding episode of the suspense drama, I fell asleep. I've no idea what happened in the end. I really don't want to ask Harry Ferris to put out the call among his listeners for anyone who might have video-recorded it. Perhaps I'll raise the subject in the canteen: I might be in luck. The sickening thing was that the music for the closing credits woke me and, like the previous night, I couldn't get to sleep for hours.

*

Jodie, the hairdressing assistant, was in the canteen this morning, uncharacteristically excited and talkative. She is reapplying to hairdressing college and is hopeful of being accepted on the full-time course, which gives her three days a week at the school salon and two days in industry. She doesn't intend to do the two days with Janice. She wants to go somewhere a bit more hip. I bet her tips won't be any better in the fashionable world. Because Janice's prices are so low, absolutely every customer responds by giving Jodie an extra one or two pound coins.

*

Hilary rang to give me Hugh Davy's phone numbers in Wales so that I can call him to arrange the meeting between him and Sally Lewis. Hilary isn't exactly delighted about the no-recording rule, but she hopes that once Sally is used to Hugh and they get to know each other, she'll agree to being recorded another day. I'm to accompany Hugh at the interview as a safety net – to remember any details he might forget. I hope this weekend suits them both.

Hilary also said she'd been speaking to the editor of Zero FM's *Artsweek* programme and had happened to mention my father was writing again. She thought they were keen to do a feature. I can almost certainly say Terry will *not* be keen.

*

We had a meeting of the Parents' Committee to progress the organisation of the summer fête. I detected a slightly lazy approach, as if, now that we have Lindy-May and Harry on board, we don't need to try so hard. But I doubt that people are going to be satisfied with a little chat to our very own celebrities if that's all there is to do. They're still going to want the barbecue and tombola, the penalty-kick competition, etc. Actually, we considered giving the tombola a miss this year because the prizes are often pointless things nobody wants and, we suspect, are frequently redonated to resume their places on the following year's stall. I know there's at least some truth in this as we won the same prize two years in a row. But it was decided, nevertheless, that if we cancelled it, people would claim they missed it, so it's staying. I've been nominated to take the begging bowl round the shops in the Riverside mall, which is all right. I'll ask Eleanor if she can look after the children for an hour one afternoon. There's no rush. The fête isn't until June.

*

I hope I sleep tonight.

* * *

This morning, a woman from an anti-littering campaign came to address us at staff training. (What this has to do with running shops, I do not know.) Basically, her message was, don't drop litter in the street or the countryside, but mind your own business and don't challenge anyone who

164

drops litter, as in this day and age there's a good chance they'll head-butt or even knife you. She made this last a good twenty minutes, during which I could see others, like myself, swallowing yawns and wiping their eyes.

At the end, the floor was thrown open for questions, but nobody asked any (probably as most of them were ninety per cent asleep). Ted Twome urged us on, but no one said anything except, eventually, Cheryl, who asked whether there were any new developments in the area of chewing-gum removal. The woman said discarded gum was an ever-increasing hazard, chewing it was a disgusting habit anyway, but if people insisted on doing it then why they couldn't wrap it up and put it into a bin she would never know. She also said there were new machines on the market to remove old gum from footpaths but they were so expensive that local councils had to think twice about buying them, especially as they were notorious for breaking down. Ted Twome thanked her on behalf of us all, but after she left the room, he went crazy, shouting his head off because nobody but Cheryl had had the courtesy to think up a suitable question for our visitor. He said we had made a very bad impression.

*

Kathleen and Lorna came in *sans* boys as Fiona is having a lieu day, which suited the grannies very well as this is Walter's birthday and they didn't think the nursing-home was the greatest place for two young children. They had come in so that Kathleen could buy candles for the birthday cake. My initial reaction to this was, 'Oh, for goodness' sake! Cake candles? Walter's nearly eighty!' But the more I think about it, the more it seems a really nice idea. I hope someone bothers to put candles on a cake for me when I'm that old.

Since Kathleen and Lorna were in anyway, they were going to look at the sandals in Shoerama and the small selection in the supermarket, for wearing in France. I suggested the usefulness of flip-flops for the beach, but Kathleen said no way. She'd had a pair of the old-style Dr Scholl's in the 1970s, and holding them on with her toes gave her terrible night pains in the backs of her thighs. Now she won't wear anything that doesn't have an ankle strap. Fair enough.

*

Mark paid us a visit to buy ink-pen cartridges in the stationer's/wannabe bookshop. He said he'd also have an espresso at the gourmet coffee place and sit at one of their tables on the walkway if I'd hang about and talk to him: he had something to show me. I said I could for a little while, providing he used the time to tell me how the drama had turned out in the end, if he had watched it, which he had. I noticed that he was again wearing his leather jacket broken-arm style, but he drank his coffee using the 'broken' arm, so it clearly wasn't impaired. I passed no remark.

After sorting out the loose ends of the suspense drama (aah! *That* explains it!), he showed me the thing he had to show me, which was some photographs he had taken at

Lindy-May's Easter Monday bash of our children with her dogs. They were beautiful. I had just pulled round a chair beside him to have a quick sit-down to study them when who should cast her shadow over us but Tanya, his tall ex-girlfriend. I now know what 'looking daggers' means. In a mutter I nevertheless heard clearly, she said, 'Thick as thieves.'

Mark either didn't hear or chose to ignore this and rose to his feet to pull out a chair for his ex, saying, 'Tanya, won't you join us?' She sat down but continued pouting. Mark asked her if she would have a coffee, which she said she would, and he went to the counter.

Tanya crossed her long legs at the knee, making it even more impossible to fit them under the table. She looked at me holding the photographs, and, suddenly, the intimacy of Mark having taken my children's pictures, at Lindy-May's house and at a party to which I don't suppose Tanya was invited, felt to me like an insult to her. I shoved the snaps into their envelope.

Tanya asked if I was off-duty. I guiltily admitted I was skiving and shouldn't be sitting at Mark's table.

He arrived back with a cappuccino, which he set before Tanya with a smile, and two Danish pastries on a plate with a spare underneath. I wondered how a man so socially graceful could possibly have a problem with anxiety, and then I noticed that, while away, he had slipped his arm back into the sleeve of his leather jacket and that this was significant. Although I strongly suspected that Mark would have liked me to stay and deflect some of Tanya's intensity, I had to get back to work. I also regretted having to decline the second Danish pastry. It was a vanilla crown, my favourite. I think Tanya was delighted when I moved off. Not because she wanted to eat both Danishes.

*

For tonight's gourmet meal, I'm roasting a whole chicken. Even I'm shocked to face the fact that, despite my many, many years as a housewife, I have never roasted an intact chicken before. In fact, I'm not sure that the children will recognise an oven-ready chicken as a chicken at all: they're used to goujons, fillet burgers and, occasionally, Kievs. (Kievs? As if a 'Kiev' was a cut of meat instead of a place in Ukraine.) Anyhow, I picked up a leaflet in the supermarket that says all you need to do is rub the chicken's breast with olive oil, then salt and pepper it, stick two halves of a lemon up its bum, and you can't go wrong. I may even put a bottle of wine in the fridge.

*

It bothers me that Tanya dislikes me. It bothers me when anyone dislikes me. I get red and heated just thinking about it. But, in Tanya's case, I don't see what I can do.

* * *

Moira Reynolds, our human-resources manager at the mall, called me into her office today. As usual, I thought I was in trouble, but no: seemingly, Moira has been booked to speak to the Country Ladies' Circle about her work at the Riverside shopping mall. She was to be their monthly guest speaker next Tuesday night. But now something's come up at her daughter Penny's school – the posh girls' school, as it happens – to do with parents supporting their children's A-level revision, and Moira feels it's more important to attend that. So, guess who she's asked to stand in for her with the Country Ladies? Me! I was more than a little surprised. I haven't even worked here a full three months yet, and I don't know much about the running of the place beyond my own job. But Moira said that was fine, she'd told them what I did, and they thought it was thrilling. Thrilling? Moira also said that the mall would pay me double time for going, and you never knew but the Country Ladies might give me something too. We're still having to watch our pennies due to facing a potentially jobless future. I couldn't turn it down.

While I was in her office, Moira also asked if I was enjoying working for the Riverside mall generally.

I said, honestly, that I thought it a good place to work. The staff were nice, the canteen and corporate-benefits package excellent. Moira seemed satisfied and suggested I could perhaps stay on in some other capacity when my time as a store detective had expired.

I felt wanted. It was nice. There is a vacancies bulletin board in the canteen. I'm going to look at it to see what's on offer. It would be a lot more comfortable working in the 'soft' environment of my local shopping mall than chasing up people who don't necessarily want to be chased for Hilary at the radio station.

*

Hugh Davy and Sally Lewis were unable to meet this weekend but are OK for next Saturday. Hugh will rendezvous with me in Mumbles coffee shop, which has a side-street car park nearby with plenty of spaces since the Riverside mall opened for business. Then I'll bring him with me to Sally Lewis's.

*

The roast chicken was a modest success. Two out of three children ate it. The third refused to accept that anything not coated in breadcrumbs counted as chicken.

*

What am I going to tell the Country Ladies' Circle about my job? I fear they'll be expecting someone more dynamic and exciting, with colourful stories to recount.

* * *

I've spent all weekend fretting about my talk to the Country Ladies' Circle. According to *him*, a fear of public speaking is the most common phobia in Western society. This news does not help. I want to use anecdotes, but they would either refer to cases of people I've caught, which might therefore be *sub judice*, or to those I've turned a blind eye to, which might, if one of the ladies blabs, get me the sack. So I'm left with nothing to say.

I phoned up Kathleen and Lorna – thinking they're the sort of women you'd find in the Circle – to ask what sort of thing they'd expect to hear. Kathleen had once been on a new-faces recruitment night with her next-door neighbour, Mrs England, who was a member. The speaker had been Jane Dare, the late-night presenter from Zero FM. Kathleen said Jane Dare had kept slugging from a dumpy bottle of Lucozade and told them she'd had an abortion for the sake of her career and had also slept with a previous controller of Zero FM for the sake of her career, and the thing she loved most about her job was the music she played, and the thing she disliked most was the matchmaker phone-in she did every Wednesday night, trying to find dates for uneasy social misfits and 'cuddly' single mothers. She shocked the Country Ladies' Circle, who were more than ready for their strong cup of tea after that but could hardly swallow their ham sandwiches. Kathleen wasn't saying that the Jane Dare experience was typical but, all the same, I notice she never went back. Lorna had no additional information. Like me, she isn't much of a joiner.

* * *

All I really want is a nice little job where I can turn up every day, do what I do, go home and, at the end of every month, there's a payment into my building-society account. And, at the end of every year, there's a roast-turkey dinner. I don't particularly want to spend my days skulking about suspecting people. I definitely don't want to cold-call people who are being looked for by shadows from their past, and right now I don't want to have to go out at night and address a hall full of people I don't know.

*

Moira gave me an hour off work this morning so she could treat me to a wash and blow-dry in Janice's salon. I might have felt insulted that she thought I required outside help with smartening up as ambassador to the Country Ladies, but I decided to feel glad: having your hair done brightens you up for the day. She also got the supermarket to assemble me a small hamper, which I was to bring to the Ladies as a prize for their monthly competition. In fact, it was Jodie who not only back-washed but also blow-dried my hair, with just a little finishing from Janice. I think she doesn't want to lose Jodie when hairdressing college starts and is hoping to tempt her into doing her work-placement days in her salon. But Jodie is young and needs to be somewhere more exciting. I see Janice has swapped her slippers for a pair of Dr Scholl's.

*

When I got to the church hall where the Country Ladies' Circle meets, I thought it smelled just a little bit fusty, but I soon discovered that the women themselves were anything but. Although there were about thirty of them, they tore through their business. There are usually only about six of us at the Parents' Committee meetings, yet it takes us hours to reach one decision.

First up with the Ladies was their summer coach trip. They already knew where they were going and what their refreshment stops would be. Now all they had to decide was whether or not to bring partners. Two women rose to argue the case for, and one spoke against. It went to a vote, and the men are to be invited.

Next item was the spring puzzle sheet. One of the Ladies had put together a page of clues with the answers given in jumbled form, which had to be figured out or deciphered. The closing date had come, and it was now time to draw a winner. The Ladies' oldest member, aged ninety, was asked to come forward and make the selection. Although a little hunched, she practically sprinted for the stage, where she drew a name to whom the president, Eileen Brogan, said she'd sold a sheet. Everyone clapped. Mrs Brogan announced that the spring puzzle sheet had raised £220 for Help the Aged. Everyone clapped again.

I was sitting on the platform beside Mrs Brogan, and my hands were now clammy, but it wasn't time for my speech yet. Next up was the monthly competition, which was entitled a Picture of Granddad. It was a clever proposition, as the younger members had brought in their favourite photographs of their grandfathers, while others, like the ninety-year-old, had pictures of their husbands or even sons, who were also granddads, doing granddaddy things. As I had brought the prize hamper, I was asked to do the judging and actually had great fun looking at the snaps, although it was terribly hard to pick a winner. Eventually, I gave the prize to a photograph of a current grandfather in his younger days, standing up in a fairground swingboat, wearing teddy-boy drapes and smoking a cigarette. I was reminded that I had never seen a photograph of Terry, my father, as a really young man – nothing before the head shot of him on his first volume of poetry (the one with 'Girl on a Gate') – and none at all of him as a boy, so I couldn't even know, for example, if any of my children resembled him as a child. I envied the women some of their pictures, but, never mind, it was a nice competition.

As I handed over the hamper, everyone clapped again, then silence fell, Eileen Brogan rose to her feet, and my heart pounded as she introduced me as the speaker.

By the time I was on my second cup of tea and my third sandwich, I concluded that there had been nothing to worry about. I had started my speech by swearing the room to secrecy, which seemed to excite them, and then told them pretty much everything that had happened since I'd started the store-detective job, leaving out names and changing a few details here and there so that no one could be identified. It wasn't so hard. They were a captive audience from the very first anecdote about the pram raid, and they gasped when I told them about the civil servant calling me the B-word and gasped again when I recounted the daylight robbery of the gold chains from Diggers.

Eileen Brogan told me that my circumnavigation of the

offending word was just about the right side of shocking for this group of women: any more explicit and they'd have rejected me. She told me they'd insisted on the then-president writing a letter of complaint to Zero FM after Jane Dare's performance, when Jane Dare had been, they suspected, drunk as she addressed them. I admitted I had heard about the incident. Eileen Brogan went on to say that Zero FM had sent them a bundle of retractable biro pens with the station logo on the side and a £50 sponsorship cheque for their next fundraising event by way of apology, but it couldn't undo the things Jane Dare had said. One elderly member had never returned.

When it was time for me to leave, Eileen Brogan thanked me and, under guise of a warm handshake, surreptitiously pressed an envelope into my grasp. I didn't look inside until I got home. It contained £25.

* * *

This morning, Moira stopped me in the corridor outside the canteen and told me that Eileen Brogan had telephoned to say how well I'd gone down at last night's meeting and to thank her for sending me. She said she wanted to give me a pat on the back and to let me know that the comment would go on my staff record. That got me thinking. Does every remark from members of the public go on our records? Is the civil servant's accusation on mine too?

*

He was so late home from work tonight that I ended up going to bed on my own. I put the radio on for company and found myself listening to the notorious Jane Dare. Not only that, but it was the night of her popular matchmaker phone-in show, which she had told the Country Ladies' Circle she despises. It's only since I met Lindy-May, Harry and Sandy that I have kept the radio tuned to Zero FM, so although Jane's lonely-hearts show has been running for years, I had never actually heard it before. Here is what happens.

First, someone who is looking for love phones in. This week it was Neville. While Jane plays 'All by Myself' by Eric Carmen in the background, Neville gets two minutes to tell the listeners about himself, prompted by Jane if he runs out of things to say and shut up by Jane if he says too much, like personal details of his children. So, we learned that Neville was thirty-six, separated for five years and divorced for three, with a boy and a girl who live with their mother and whom he sees on alternate weekends. He teaches woodwork at two local further-education colleges, where he's also one of the staff first-aiders. There he got stuck. With coaxing from Jane, he went on to say that he's straight, plays golf once a week on the municipal course, enjoys watching football and snooker on TV, once tried judo but didn't like it, lives in his own small three-bedroom terraced house with no garden, doesn't have any pets and doesn't want any and can't really swim.

I couldn't switch it off. It was oddly compelling. Jane

played a few more songs while they waited for the return calls to come in and the callers to be selected and prepared before they went on air. Then we got to hear the three chosen replies.

First up was Norma. Over a background track of 'Love Story', Norma had one minute to recommend herself, which she did by saying that she was tallish and slim with long, curly hair – permed, Jane Dare got her to reveal – and she, too, was divorced for some years, with one child who lived with her but who was close to its grandparents. She, too, enjoyed watching sport on television and was also, in fact, a swimming instructor: she would happily give Neville lessons if he wished.

Jane thanked Norma and went back to Neville who, I'd thought, would be thrilled by such a portrait. But he didn't jump at the first offer, as the format seemingly allows. Rather, he elected to hear the other two options before he made up his mind.

We moved on to Josie. Here, Jane had her work cut out, and I saw why she might dislike this weekly feature. With much coaxing, over a background track of 'Feelings', Josie eventually volunteered that she was forty, thirteen stone, probably had agoraphobia and definitely had a deaf Jack Russell terrier called Disney (he'll never know, unless he can lip-read). Norma certainly had the edge so far.

Then Jane Dare reminded us of the deal. Once Neville had picked a winner, the radio station would treat them to a three-course meal at Maison Philippe, they'd see how they got on and come back in two weeks to report on how things had unfolded.

Before we met the third contestant for Neville's affections, we went to an interview with the winners from a fortnight ago, a PA and a digger driver, who said they'd had a 'brilliant' time at Maison Philippe, where the food had been 'brilliant', and equally 'brilliant' were the staff, and that all round it had been a 'brilliant' opportunity but, sadly, one they wouldn't be repeating as they hadn't really clicked as a couple. Jane Dare first made disappointed noises, then sort of cooing, coaxing sounds, as if she could persuade them by her own efforts that their mismatch could be resolved. But it turned out to be OK because the PA had already introduced the digger driver to a friend of hers who worked as a project manager on building sites, and they were getting on like a house on fire, so all was not lost.

Then it was back to tonight's matchmaking and caller number three.

She introduced herself over 'Without You'. She had a deeply husky, slightly nasal voice and said her name was Pamela; she was a thirty-five-year-old receptionist in a BMW garage. She drove a BMW, a black one, and, in her opinion, BMWs were the best cars in the world. She was allergic to animal fur and pollen, but she kept this well under control with antihistamines. She was a size ten in clothes and a size four and a half in shoes and she had long, black hair. She wore suits with blouses to work but jeans and casual tops at home.

Jane Dare asked cheekily whether she wore stockings or tights with her work suits.

Pamela said, 'Oh, stockings,' in a voice that implied she wouldn't dream of wearing anything else.

Guess who Neville picked. Jane thanked Norma and Josie for taking part and told Neville and Pamela to stay on the line: someone would explain to them the arrangements for visiting Maison Philippe. She then played 'Sheena Is a Punk Rocker', which she'd clearly been dying to do all night, and I stayed awake for a while but heard no mice scraping. I tried to picture a bestockinged Pamela driving Neville to the municipal golf course in her black BMW and came to the conclusion that, on this one, Neville had overreached himself.

* * *

Ted Twome is either inspired or a bit mad, judging by this morning's training session. The visiting speaker looked unremarkable. She was wearing black slacks over black boots, with a white, pink and black blouse that looked like one I saw in the window of the Edinburgh Woollen Mill. She'd a large, good-quality carrier-bag with her, the kind made of toughened paper with rope handles, which she set on the chair behind her. Ted Twome merely introduced her as 'Anthea' and said she was there this morning to try us with something completely different and that he would let her do the explaining. What could it be?

Anthea called us 'ladies and gentlemen' and teased us by

telling us she had a clue in her carrier-bag that would probably give away why she was there. I don't think anyone could have guessed what was in it or been more surprised when it turned out to be a fringed pink cowgirl hat. Anthea was a line-dancing teacher.

There was a sort of collective disbelieving laugh, then a bit of a rumble, glances at each other and some eye-rolling as we realised this was actually happening – we were going to be line-dancing in the staff training room of the Riverside shopping mall at nine o'clock in the morning. And the thing is, even allowing for the Shania Twain CD, it was really good fun! As Ted Twome collected in our evaluation sheets at the end of the session, he kept remarking how happy and smiley we all were, and he was right.

Later in the canteen Cheryl, the PR girl with the hourglass figure, told us that line-dancing burns up the same number of calories as cycling at ten miles per hour. This equivalent to a five-mile bike ride might have done us more good, though, if we hadn't rushed to the canteen afterwards for Mars bars.

*

My father rang me this afternoon. He never rings me. He wanted to know if I'll look at his new poems as he's considering sending them to his old publisher but needs to know if they're any good. I asked him if he couldn't show them to my mother, and he said he would, but he wanted me to see them first.

These are his first poems in twenty years. How could I refuse? Now I'm afraid that (a) I will not understand them, or (b) I'll understand them, but they'll be no good, or (c) I'll think they're good when they're not. Of course, the obvious person to send them to would be Marcus, my father's old editor, who always used to send us children Christmas selection boxes in January. Sadly, and inconveniently, he is dead.

* * *

Today, Lindy-May was back in the canteen. I thought she was still a bit off with me, but I ploughed on anyhow. I told her about hearing Jane Dare's lonely-hearts feature for the first time, which at least elicited a smile. Lindy-May said she and Harry used to listen to it in bed, which made me wonder, not for the first time, what their domestic arrangements are. Then I told her what I'd heard about Jane at the Country Ladies' Circle, with the Lucozade and the abortion, and Lindy-May sighed and said that was Jane, all right, and the clouds came over her face again and she returned to flipping the pages of her celebrity magazine. But I can't afford to worry about Lindy-May too much. I'm already worrying about meeting Hugh Davy tomorrow, then bringing him to see Sally Lewis.

* * *

I'm exhausted. And if I'm exhausted, how must Hugh Davy be feeling? It's his life, after all. He's staying in a hotel tonight. A proper grown-up would have asked him back to their place for sustenance and company, but our home isn't like others. It's all crumby and black-fingerprinty and chipped paint, and we don't even have a normal tray for serving tea and coffee, just a big lumpy plastic one with Santa on it. No. I couldn't invite Hugh into that. Anyhow, he returns to Wales tomorrow, and it's his family he'll want to be with while he digests his information, not a stranger like me.

I don't think today went quite as he had expected. I, for one, was surprised to discover that Sally Lewis had assembled a whole posse for the visit. I don't know who they were. A mixture of friends, neighbours and relatives, I think. I reckon there were five in the house, but as they kept going in and out of the kitchen for the teapot, etc., I couldn't be sure. Sally Lewis was a rather strange woman. She didn't answer the door herself, so when we walked in she was smoking a cigarette in a chair that seemed very much her chair, facing the telly – it wasn't switched on – with a small glass ashtray on the arm. She wore a large cardigan, which she pulled tighter round her several times while we were there, and she kept her cigarettes and lighter in one of the patch pockets. She wore lipstick, powder and comfortable fleece-lined slippers.

Hugh has nice manners and shook hands with everyone as he encountered them. I did the same less confidently. When he went into the room where Sally was, she didn't rise to greet him but took his hand when he extended it and said quietly that she was glad to see him. She isn't a particularly small woman, but she had a frailness about her, and I thought it fortunate that Hugh had decided to seek her out sooner rather than later: although still just in her sixties, she has the appearance of a woman in decline.

After refreshments were insisted upon and distributed by Sally's helpers, Hugh told her about finding the article in the paper but asked her if she would tell him face to face what she'd witnessed the night he was found. She did. There was nothing new, and she soon moved on to tell Hugh how happy she was to hear that he had gone on to have a good life, and that she'd often thought of him as time went by. She asked if she could see photographs of his wife and children, and Hugh produced some from his wallet, which Sally looked at for a long time.

Then, as if it was nothing, she revealed that, at the time the news broke about Baby Noel's discovery, several people had told her that a young woman in a long black overcoat had been seen about the place on the day in question, speaking in the distinctive accent of a little seaside town not far away. One person had even said she'd been asking for directions to the church where Hugh Davy was abandoned. Unfortunately, Sally was unable to produce the originators of these testimonies – they were either dead or gone.

When it seemed certain that there was nothing further she could tell him, we rose to leave, and Hugh again extended his hand. Again, Sally took and shook it. Why didn't she just hug him? They both wanted her to.

Everybody was nice to Hugh, who was the centre of the story. Everyone was cold to me, because I was the parasite from the radio station, looking to capitalise on someone else's situation.

When I got home, I had to write down everything I could remember about the interview for use in the programme as no recording had been allowed. Hilary rang me at about ten thirty – getting me out of bed, doesn't she understand? – and asked me to relate what had been said. I did so.

I didn't say this, because Hilary didn't ask, but I didn't believe everything Sally Lewis said. I don't think she did find an abandoned baby. I think she's covering for someone. I think she's covering for Hugh's mother.

* * *

Today, Jodie was the centre of attention in the canteen. She was wearing a new pair of sandals, which even I could see were beautiful. They're called 'Carnival', and she'd bought them in Jill's shop. They're quite flat and look like a Ferris wheel of tan leather and beads. They also come in white and in silver, Jodie said. Everybody wants a pair. Of course, it helps that Jodie's feet look as good as they do. She has had her toes done in a French manicure style at the new nail bar in Janice's salon.

*

The Television Awards of the Year are on telly tonight, hosted by Sir Trevor McDonald. The ceremony took place yesterday, so the key results have already been revealed on this morning's breakfast-news bulletins. Lorcan Hinds won Best Male in a Dramatic Performance, for *Mac*. Unlike several others, he returned from America to pick up the award in person. I've seen a short clip, and he still looks 'devastatingly handsome'. I'll watch the full thing later.

*

What does Cheryl do all day? It's been weeks since the bonny-baby competition.

*

Terry has been on again, asking me to read his new poems. I said I'd call and get them tomorrow on my way home from work. Oh dearie dear. I don't want this task.

* * *

Terrible news! It was on Zero FM that a rat has bitten a child at Peter Piper's Soft Adventure Play Barn! The child was playing in the pit of plastic balls when the attack took place. I'm full of the horrors. My listening for mouse scratches in our house has turned to listening for rat scratches. My family couldn't care less. The children think it would have been 'cool' to be the child who was bitten. What's the matter with them? (Am I the only person in the entire town to be rendered jittery by this event?)

*

I've tried to read Terry's poems. They worry me. I think they might be very good, but I also think they might be saying that Eleanor has ruined his life.

*

My only delight in an otherwise joyless day came when I picked up the new *Radio Times* to see that next week's Andrew Duncan interview is with a home-for-the-holidays Lorcan Hinds.

* * *

Our house is so untidy, with little piles of debris everywhere. It's the perfect hideout for a rat. I'm almost obsessively emptying the kitchen bin and wiping up crumbs, but the children insist on taking biscuits upstairs and leaving their school trousers lying about, the pockets stuffed with foody lunch wrappings. In an effort to take my mind off matters rodent, I forced myself to go to bed, lie down and listen to Jane Dare's programme. It's the night for her lonely hearts again. Of course, this time *he* was lying beside me and my innocent enjoyment of the previous week was altered because he was thinking what a stupid programme it was. So, I couldn't really savour plus-size Marcella, who works in corporate banking and has more than seventy pairs of shoes, as she tried to sort the sheep from the goats between Martin, a pig farmer, Nigel, who had seen *Buddy!* the musical seven times, and Steve, an accountant who claimed to look like Phil Mitchell. I could feel the vibes in the bed beside me, saying, 'Good grief,' and I felt stupid for enjoying such 'entertainment'. (Marcella went for Steve.)

*

Two of the checkout girls were wearing 'Carnival' sandals today. I'm glad of the business for Jill.

* * *

I've got myself into such a mess by letting my emotions get the better of me. It started right after staff training when Janice came storming out of her salon and accosted me in the corridor. She was really angry, red and fuming, and jabbing the point of her tail-comb at my face. The gist of it? Who did I think I was, interfering in Jodie's plans for where she was going to do her industry placement once she starts hairdressing college?

As we all know, Janice wants Jodie to come to her, but Jodie wants to go somewhere younger and more 'with it'. In the canteen the other day, after all the excitement over the sandals, the talk may have turned to Jodie's plans, and I may have said something to the effect that she had to choose what was best for her and not necessarily do what Janice wanted – but everybody was saying it. It was a general consensus, not just me.

That clearly wasn't the impression Janice had formed. She was singling me out to carry the blame. And she more or less dared me ever to return to her salon, if I wanted to see what she would do to my hair. There were people about, who stood and stared, which made the incident all the more embarrassing. I went to the toilets in the locker room to collect myself, took deep breaths and managed not to cry. I then eschewed the staff-and-goods lift in favour of the stairs to buy myself more calming-down time.

When I had walked off a little of my upset, I managed to work up a tad of righteous indignation, and therein – oh dear, therein – the danger lay. It wasn't long before who should show up but the shoplifter in the uniform of the posh girls' school. She made her usual entrance, gliding in through the automatic doors, then dancing her coquettish little dance around Leon, which involved much pulling up of her falling-down socks, flicking her hair and changing her neat, fashionable schoolbag from shoulder to shoulder. Then she floated off in the direction of Pharmacity.

This time, maintaining a discreet distance, I followed her. I didn't have long to wait for her to make a move: soon she was slipping an eyeshadow into her blazer pocket, then a nail varnish. She left the shop and crossed the walkway to the stationer's/wannabe bookshop, where she calmly slipped a copy of *Cosmopolitan* into her bag. How could she be so blatant?

I looked round for assistance but, as expected, Tony and Leon were nowhere to be seen, and the shop assistant was dealing with customers at the till. Then I thought I'd try making my presence felt, as Tony had done with the pocket-guide thief, and maybe she'd put the stuff back voluntarily.

But when I went and stood near her, she did something that made the colour rise in my cheeks: she made a V shape with her index and middle fingers and slid them up the side of her face that was turned to me, as though she were merely supporting her cheek when really she was showing me a two-fingered salute. Well! On top of my existing bed of righteous indignation, this was too much. Without thinking through any consequences, I marched off to get Moira Reynolds, who, I felt sure, wouldn't stand for any nonsense. I didn't even wait for the lift – I took the stairs two at a time and sped towards her office.

Fortuitously, Moira was winding up a bit of work and not too busy to see me. I spat out what was happening and did everything but take her hand and drag her downstairs to confront the girl. To my delight, Moira seemed as indignant as I was at the news of the girl's audacious looting. She swept us out of her office to deal with the matter once and for all. There was just one thing, though. She'd arranged to meet someone in the canteen and had to pop her head in to let them know she was going to be held up. I could hardly bear it! If we didn't get downstairs quickly, the posh girl shoplifter would have flown! So, imagine how I felt when Moira opened the canteen door and who was standing at the serving hatch but the posh girl shoplifter herself, to whom Moira Reynolds said, 'Hello, Penny, I'm just going to be five minutes,' and who replied, 'Hi, Mum! No problem!'

*

189

Terry wants to know what I think of the poems. If I say I don't like them, will I break his spirit? But if I say I do like them, and he submits them for publication, will it break Eleanor's heart?

*

Peter Piper's Soft Adventure Play Barn has been temporarily closed down by health inspectors after a rats' nest was found.

*

I'm jumpy as hell.

*

I had to go down in the staff-and-goods lift with Moira and pretend to look for the posh girl shoplifter, even though I knew she was upstairs in the canteen. Why couldn't I have done as everyone else did and turn a blind eye for the sake of my job? What should I do now? Afterwards, Moira actually sat me down at the canteen table with Penny, who was having hot chocolate with marshmallows, and introduced her as 'My baby', a title in which her daughter proudly basked. She even asked Penny's advice – Moira was trying to find out if her daughter might know the identity of the culprit.

Cool as a cucumber, Penny appeared to consider the possibilities but came back with the answer that the description could apply to any one of many. She flashed me a glinty-eyed smile that acknowledged I'd had the opportunity to shop her but hadn't dared to take it once I knew who she was, and now it was too late.

But I knew I'd rattled her comfort zone, if only for a few minutes, by getting her mother involved, and I suspected she'd find a way to make me pay. Little does Moira know that her daughter's reasons for wanting to become a forensic psychologist may be on the dark side – she's already a small-town criminal mastermind. And what about all the stuff I'd said to Moira about the rest of the security staff looking the other way when the girl came around? Is she going to confront them with these accusations, and is she going to name me as the source?

*

Plus, Hilary has been on to me again, wanting me to go back to see Sally Lewis and probe her a bit more on the events of the night Baby Noel was found. Hilary doesn't seem to understand the nervy sort of woman Sally Lewis is. She won't appreciate being badgered. Hilary also wants me to go to the little seaside town where one line of thought alleges Hugh's birth mother came from to see if I can find any leads. After thirty-five years? Where the hell does she expect me to start?

* * *

Good news and bad news. The bad news is that Sally Lewis told me off for ringing her again last night. She said she's said all she can say and now wishes to be left alone. I told her

I was just trying to help Hugh find his mother, but she pointed out that I was only helping him because I was being paid to do so. All the same, I told her I worked in the Riverside mall in the mornings but that she could reach me by phone in the afternoons and evenings if she thought of anything. I don't think she even wrote down the number.

The good news is that Kathleen and Lorna came into the mall today. They started off by telling me I looked tired and asking if anything was wrong. Where would I start? The rats? The poems? Lindy-May going cold on me? Tanya loathing me? Sally Lewis and her posse regarding me as a parasite? Janice hating me? The civil-servant shoplifter wanting to damage my reputation? Penny Reynolds looking for payback? My colleagues possibly about to ostracise me? How has it come to this? But with Kathleen and Lorna, at least, I'm regarded as a reasonable and even a nice person. And the good news about their visit is that Kathleen has an old friend who lives in the seaside town from which Baby Noel's suspected birth mother supposedly came, and this friend is, even if Kathleen says it herself, really quite a nosy-parker who makes everyone's business her own. If there's anything to be known about a girl from the town having a secret baby in 1972, then she's the very woman to know about it. Joy! A lead!

*

After work, as I was walking to my car, I felt as if someone was following me. I refused to allow myself to look round –

that would have been paranoid behaviour – but I picked up my pace and dug my keys out of my handbag as I went, then practically leaped into the car.

* * *

At a time when things aren't going particularly well for me, Kathleen and Lorna are ever more my guardian angels. They were complete sweethearts about my excursion to the seaside to see Kathleen's nosy friend, who is called Myrtle, and not only came with me, having packed a picnic for afterwards, but stayed throughout the interview.

Myrtle lives in a retirement bungalow with her husband Norman, who was out playing crown green bowls as he is every morning, which Myrtle approves of because she can't have him under her feet while she's doing the household chores. They have a view of the sand dunes from their front window, but not of the sea, two grown-up sons, who live elsewhere, and a little Yorkshire terrier called Baby.

Myrtle made us tea in china beakers, offered us scones and Jamaica ginger cake and asked me, as though I were aged seven, if I'd rather she got me a chocolate biscuit. Baby followed her every movement, scampering in such a way that I thought he'd be a lot more dangerous underfoot than Norman could possibly be, but Myrtle just made affectionate-frustration noises and didn't seem to mind.

Kathleen had warned me that Myrtle was the nosiest person on the planet and I was sure to get the full interrogation, but I was to tell her nothing and get on with my business. All the same, before I could get out a single question about Baby Noel, Myrtle had established my age, my children's ages, what *he* does for a living, how long we've been living in our house and how much we reckon it has appreciated in value since we moved in. To be fair, she told us freely what she and Norman had paid for their bungalow and that its value had gone up by four hundred per cent since they'd bought it, but that this hardly mattered as Gordon Brown would end up selling it out from under them in a few years to pay their fees in a retirement home. She seemed resigned to this.

When we finally got to the story of Hugh Davy's arrival in the world, Myrtle was quite clear: at the time the story had appeared in the newspaper and on the local television and radio news, everyone in her town had sat up and pricked their ears at the suggestion that the young mother was a local. The talk had gone round the place like wildfire, and it wasn't long before the conclusion followed that there wasn't a single suggestion in the entire place that any girl had secretly given birth to a baby and that such a thing could never be so completely covered up. The people of the town simply dismissed the possibility as a tale told by Sally Lewis, and the speculation then was that she was covering for a younger sister or niece who had found herself 'in trouble'. I asked Myrtle how definite people had been about this, and she said four hundred per cent definite, and that you couldn't keep a secret in a town this size for thirty-five minutes, never mind thirty-five years.

Kathleen told Myrtle I wasn't myself today because I was having worries about mice and rats about my house, even though I didn't know if we had a real problem or it was just in my mind. Myrtle said I should get a Yorkshire terrier like her Baby as they were devils for mice and rats and she hadn't seen a thing about the place since she'd started keeping Baby or his predecessor, Midge. I know we've always supported a no-pets rule at home, based on the fact that the children already take so much looking after, but if I thought a small terrier could guarantee a rodent-free zone, the daily walking and turd duty would seem a small price to pay.

As we drove away, Myrtle held up Baby at the front window and waved his paw at us.

We managed to find a space in a car park overlooking the sea. Myrtle had told us that hardly anyone comes to the beach on Saturdays now because they're doing retail therapy instead. For our picnic, Kathleen and Lorna had brought egg-mayonnaise sandwiches, grated-cheese and tomato sandwiches, chocolate tea-cakes and a tartan flask of tea. It was a bit blowy so we had it in the car.

* * *

Today, Tony and Leon were still fine with me, so Moira Reynolds mustn't have said anything yet about what I told her regarding turning a blind eye.

*

I left a message on Hilary's answering-service telling her what Myrtle had said about the young mother definitely not coming from her town.

* * *

I could hardly wait for my morning break so that I could read the Andrew Duncan interview with Lorcan Hinds in the *Radio Times*. It turns out that Lorcan Hinds has finished his work in Hollywood, where he was staying in a property owned by Sophia Loren, and is now back in the United Kingdom for some time to come. He is returning to the theatre because of a new project he has been offered by a director he worships. It's a production of *Macbeth*, with him in the lead role. But the twist is that two very different leading ladies will play opposite him on alternate nights. Francesca Annis will play Lady Macbeth as an older-woman, scheming, last-chance-for-greatness wife, and Billie Piper will play her as a sort of heartless child bride who hasn't yet developed a conscience. Lorcan Hinds said that this was what made the production so intriguing to him and was the reason he'd agreed to do it. He didn't list all the tour venues, but I hope it comes to somewhere near us. (I'd like to see both versions.)

Lorcan Hinds said he couldn't live full-time in the US because he'd miss too many things, such as pubs, sausages, the FA Cup Final and the Grand National. He also said he wasn't cut out for the Los Angeles culture of omnipresent pulsating ambition. He said he likes to choose his company on the basis of shared interests, not on the basis of who can give you a leg up the ladder. All the same, he agreed that he'd had offers of movie work, some of which he may accept.

Andrew Duncan implied that he asked Lorcan about his rumoured relationship with Beth Marsh, but that the actor would acknowledge only that Beth was a great talent with a bright future in the movie industry in the States, and that they had been great pals while he'd been over there. So, gallant *and* discreet.

*

Hilary has left a message on my phone asking me to ring her.

* * *

Walter's sister, Maureen, bought him new pyjamas from the supermarket in the mall for his birthday, as did Kathleen. Unlike Kathleen, Walter's sister doesn't visit him often enough to know that he has put on weight due to nursing-home food and only being able to walk with the aid of a frame, so her pair was too small. Kathleen brought them in to see if she could change them, which she can, except they've run out of the larger size so she'll have to wait for them to come back into stock. It has been arranged that when they come in, the supermarket girls will give them to me to give to Kathleen. This makes me feel useful and also as if I belong. It's a pity that my tenure here is about to explode when it's found out that I grassed up my colleagues over shoplifter Penny.

*

I overheard in the canteen today (chicken and ham pie with salad, £1.40) that Jodie has got her place at hairdressing college and that her industry placement is at the Waterfront on Canal Street, the coolest salon in town. I carefully stayed out of the conversation.

Gemma, one of the assistants from Diggers Discount Jewellery, has got herself a pair of 'Carnival' sandals in white. Two more of the supermarket girls have them in tan.

*

Hilary wants me to go back and see Myrtle again but with a sound recordist alongside me. She says it's no problem if Myrtle says categorically that Baby Noel's mother was not from her town. She says it's all part of the unfolding story. I said I didn't know if Myrtle would agree to going on the record, and Hilary says we can leave out her identity, if that makes her amenable, and credit her as 'a woman who has been at the centre of her community for forty years.' All the same, I'll sound out Kathleen before I approach Myrtle. I told Hilary it'll have to be on Saturday. She said she'd put it in the sound recordist's diary.

*

I phoned Kathleen as soon as I got in from work and she said she didn't think Myrtle would be at all put off by being on the radio, especially if she could say her piece incognito. Then she said what I'd been hoping she'd say: that she would ring Myrtle and ask her, if I wanted. It's not a nice job, asking people to do things they may not wish to do, and I was practically dripping with gratitude. Within fifteen minutes, Kathleen had rung back to say Myrtle was fine with the recording, as long as we didn't use her name. Hallelujah.

*

In the nick of time, I remembered to switch on Jane Dare's matchmaking programme to hear how single dad Neville and BMW-driving Pamela had got on at Maison Philippe. Of course, that entailed listening to this week's lonely hearts first, which is how they suck you in to keeping tuning in, because now I'll have to return in yet another two weeks to hear how Aaron, a home-heating oil-delivery driver, who sings in a country music band at the weekends, gets on with Paula, a hospital cook, with interests in kick-boxing and sugarcraft.

When we finally got round to the couple from a fortnight ago, Jane asked Neville what his first impression had been of Pamela on meeting her in the flesh. Neville said it had been how very good-looking Pamela was. Jane then asked Pamela the same question, to which Pamela replied that she'd first noticed Neville's lovely shoes. Draw your own conclusions. Neville went on to reveal that he had found much more that was attractive about Pamela: her husky voice, her smoky eyes, her cloud of loose, dark hair. Pamela went on to reveal that she'd just come out of a long engagement and had felt, after the Maison Philippe experience, that she wasn't ready to embark on another serious relationship. Poor Neville. Dumped. On air.

* * *

At staff training this morning, we learned how to build more exercise into our daily routines. For example, when we're hanging washing on the line, instead of just bending down and reaching up once for each item, we should do three squats and three reaches with every garment. It also means not parking your car in the mall's car park but leaving it on the far side of town, then walking to and from it. In my case, this means parking beside the canal, near Mark's old flat, walking along Canal Street, Castle Rise, Park Street and finally Riverside Lane to get to work and, obviously, the same thing in reverse on the way back.

*

I don't know whether to tell them, particularly as Kathleen is (a) a homophobe and (b) one of the few friends I may soon have left, but the staff in the young-fashions shop think she and Lorna are a same-sex couple. This arose because they were in the shop this morning looking for denim jeans for Kathleen for France. (Jeans! For Kathleen! This would have been news enough.) Seemingly, Kathleen had been delighted because the young-fashions shop did petite sizes, and she is only about five feet one, but a problem arose because of the stiffness of the new stud button at the waist and Kathleen's slightly arthritic hands. The assistant asked whether she would like some help, or if she would prefer her 'partner', meaning Lorna, who was loitering nearby, to assist. And Kathleen, merely repeating what was being said and without a clue what was meant, requested, 'My partner, please.' So, Lorna was shepherded behind the changing-room curtain, and the shop staff said how marvellous they were. As everybody now knows the grannies are my friends, I was asked if they had gone through a civil-partnership ceremony, which was how the story came out.

*

The sound recordist phoned to ask if it was all right with me if we used his car to get to Myrtle's on Saturday. I said it was fine. I felt like asking if it was all right with him if I brought two elderly ladies and a picnic, but I know I must do this one on my own.

* * *

A big new factory-outlet park is coming to the village where Mark Strain has his antiques and collectibles shop. It was in the local paper and now on Zero FM news. It's going to be a new-build project and is expected to create more than fifty jobs. It'll be open by Christmas. Anyone who knows that sleepy little village must feel some sense of loss at the prospect of it being ploughed up for new roadways and erections, but even people who live in sleepy little villages need jobs.

According to the local paper, goods on offer will include

fashions, footwear, household textiles, garden furniture and 'dining'.

Aren't building sites a favourite haunt of rats?

* * *

Today's outing to the seaside with the sound recordist was an education. We spent a full hour before we went near Myrtle capturing the aural landscape. First, we went to the end of the pier to get the sounds of waves crashing against concrete. Then we went to the harbour and caught the seagulls' shrieks. Then we went to the arcade to get the sound of a jackpot being paid out. Actually, we cheated a little on that one and recorded the sound of fifty 2ps cascading out of a change machine, but it sounded more like a jackpot than the actual jackpot. These were all 'establishing sounds', the recordist explained, to set the scene for this part of the story.

I wondered what sounds we would use to 'establish' Myrtle: that of an elderly man closing the front door on his way out to play crown green bowls? The yapping of a small Yorkshire terrier? Actually, we recorded the doorbell, which was particularly sonorous, the kettle boiling and Myrtle making a pot of tea, so I wasn't far out.

Once again, Myrtle told me how the tale of Baby Noel's mother had swept the town and how, quite indignantly, the locals felt they had been scapegoated by someone wanting to lay a false trail, not caring what questions or accusations this might stir up for the innocent. She was more emphatic than ever: Hugh Davy's young birth mother had not come from their town. (We asked her not to repeat her earlier speculation that Sally Lewis must have a young relative for whom she was covering, as this might get us into trouble. But, as Hilary had told us, that didn't mean we wouldn't follow it up.)

After the formal interview, Myrtle asked me if I had started sleeping any better, and I admitted I had not. Proudly, but not unsympathetically, she told me she was a great sleeper and had never had any such trouble. She suggested a lavender pillow, by which one of her late aunts had sworn. Since the rats thing, I sleep – or, rather, don't sleep – with a duvet tucked in all the way round me, like a sausage roll, full to the throat with camomile tea. I don't see a lavender pillow making any significant difference. I could almost have cried, out of weariness or because I was so touched, when Myrtle told me that if my sleeping didn't improve I could do worse than try the sea air. Everyone slept well at the seaside, and she had a lovely guest bedroom, all done in lemon, that I was very welcome to use.

* * *

First thing this morning, when I was in the locker room, Moira Reynolds stuck her head round the door, spotted me and asked me briskly to come up to her office when I was ready. Everybody looked at me, and I saw myself blush in the mirror as I finished combing my hair. One of the checkout girls asked if I was in trouble. I said frankly, 'I don't know.'

It turned out that it was, indeed, to do with my accusations. Moira had lined up CCTV footage of the day in question and instead of patrolling the mall I was to spend my time viewing the recordings to see if I could point out the culprit. The equipment was in Moira's office, so I had to sit there, in full view of the mother, while scrutinising, or pretending to scrutinise, the recordings for – unknown to her – images of the daughter. Moira didn't say what she had done, or intended to do, about addressing what I had said of other staff turning a blind eye. I wished I could read her mind.

As I sat there, watching and waiting, my mind continued to whirl as it had done all night – had done every night for ages, actually: *his* job, my job, Penny, Lindy-May, Tanya, poems, rodents, Penny, motherless children, nervous Sally, Penny, Penny – Penny!

There she was on the screen, just coming in through the automatic doors, stopping with Leon, doing her little dance, pulling up her socks, flicking her hair. All as I had witnessed it. Her gliding looked a bit less fluid on tape. Then on into Pharmacity, where she was suddenly lost to the camera but, of course, being Moira's daughter and having been in this office, she would know that.

After Moira had finished her piece of work, she came round and stood behind me, little knowing that her culprit daughter had just ducked into the stationer's/wannabe bookshop and out of camera range. Moira asked if I'd had any luck, and I lied that I'd found nothing. She then said the words I'd been fearing: that she would have to share my accusation with the rest of the security staff, as it affected them too, and off she went. I didn't know if she'd use my name, or leave them to guess that I had spilled the poisoned beans.

I took my morning break at some length, with Moira out of the way, but sat by myself in the training room, for fear of bumping into Tony or Leon in the canteen. Then I returned to Moira's office where I looked at the tapes, pointlessly, all over again, eking it out until lunchtime when I packed up and set off for home.

And so, after yet another sleepless night and jittery morning at work, headed for another rat-fearing afternoon, I was walking across the car park (where, despite recent health and fitness advice, I've lazily persisted in parking the car), when I thought I could see something unexpected on the bonnet. But it wasn't actually on the bonnet, I realised, as I drew closer. It was on the windscreen. Sprayed on the windscreen. It was graffiti. Not paint, I perceived, as I approached and poked it with my finger, but squirty UHT cream. Just one word. BITCH.

Part Three

In and Out

The immediate problem was: how to clean off the cream so that I could drive home. I peered hopefully into my handbag where I found a packet containing one Handy Andy. That wasn't even going to look at the job. I knew I couldn't put on the wipers and squirt the jet of water because that would smear an emulsion across the glass and I wouldn't be able to see out at all. So, I had the ignominy of getting into my soiled car, like a corruption of a 'Just Married' limo, and driving very carefully, peering round and through the big cream letters, to the hot-foam car-wash.

I couldn't have enjoyed it less. I sat in my silent bubble, with the windows up tight, while the attendants worked wordlessly round me. (Surely they'd talk about my crude window message when I'd gone.) And then, after they had sudsed, scrubbed and showered me, after I had opened my door, reluctantly, and paid them with a minimum of eye contact, I tried, and failed, to drive off. What a time for water in the electrics. At that moment, I wished I could cry, wished the floodgates would open and two cascading rivers of tears would course down my cheeks. But I had passed that stage. I felt like a screw that was being ever tightened and that if I was turned just one more time I'd bust.

I stepped dizzily out of the car and asked if I could use my phone before they pushed me out of sight as they had the last time. I rang Eleanor, who was at home, thank God, and asked her to do the school pick-ups as I was stranded. She asked me if I was all right. I replied that I was. Well, it's what you say, isn't it?

*

Who has done this to me? I mean, four months ago I didn't have an enemy in the world, as far as I know. Now it seems I've nothing but.

*

It has crossed my mind to bring the matter to the police, but it isn't a crime for Special Branch, is it? Harassment by whipped cream? Is it more of a consumer issue? In which case perhaps I should be approaching the Citizens' Advice Bureau.

* * *

In bed, early this morning, I heard scrabbling coming from the attic. *He* says it's just birds on the roof, but I'm not so sure.

I don't want to go to work, but I'm afraid to stay home. *Is* it just birds on the roof?

*

I've lost the nerve to do my job. I thought I saw a woman stuff a cardigan into her shopping-bag in the discount designer store, but I was so assailed by self-doubt I was afraid to trust my judgement. And I don't know whether Tony and Leon are still working with me, or if they've been informed of my betrayal. Oh, how I regret losing my cool and starting this ball rolling about Penny.

* * *

Kathleen and Lorna were in today, asking me whether they should buy some fake tan for the beach at France. How should I know? (Now I'm so tired I'm even getting crotchety with my only remaining friends. This can't go on.) I made sure they understood that fake tan doesn't give you any protection against sunburn and then said it was up to them. I could see it working for Lorna, whose skin tone leans naturally towards golden, but on Kathleen, who is pale and chalky like me, it'll look like smeared-on cocoa. They invited me to go to the Tasty Ranch for lunch with them and the boys after my shift, but I declined. I'm off my food.

*

Parents' Committee meeting tonight. I was asked how I was getting on rounding up tombola prizes from the shops in the Riverside mall. I admitted I hadn't yet begun. Nobody chastised me, but I could feel the swell of disapproval. How I wish I hadn't volunteered to do this or had sorted it out with the shops *before* I began alienating everybody.

*

Eleanor has offered to take the children swimming tomorrow. I think she suspects I'm not well. She doesn't deserve the poems Terry wrote.

* * *

Walter's replacement pyjamas came in today. One of the supermarket girls brought them to me as I was mooning about near the staff-and-goods lift on my morning break. I put them in my locker, then forgot to bring them home for Kathleen.

* * *

Today, I've been in three places I did not expect to be: a cuddle party, an accident and emergency department and a psychiatric building. I might as well start at the start.

As has been the case all week, I struggled through my morning at the mall, unsure where I stood with my colleagues, trying to blend in with the paintwork and careful not to start anything. I didn't go to the canteen at my morning break, just sat in an empty cubicle in the women's staff toilets beside the locker room. When it was time to go home, I got my stuff from my locker and could have kicked myself for having chosen *this* morning to park a brisk walk away.

Even as I left the mall car park, I felt slightly self-conscious, and along Riverside Lane I had the creepy sensation that I was being followed. On a better day – i.e., a day when I was not feeling persecuted, despised, exhausted, outcast and beyond tears – I might have stopped and looked round to see who, if anyone, was there. But this was not a better day, and I just kept on walking.

When I crossed the way to get to Park Road, the feeling was growing stronger, and I felt sure that someone had crossed the street behind me. I walked faster, imagining that the person was coming close enough to reach out and tap my shoulder – and then what? Would I turn round to be punched squarely between the eyes? I was starting to panic, and the only salvation I could see was to get off that road before something bad happened. Which was how I came to seek sanctuary through the only open door I could see, which happened to be Brian and Sheelagh's old house and was now the territory of a reiki healer and sometime cuddle-party host. I practically threw myself in and, on closing the inner door behind me, I experienced the fragrance of jasmine, the soothing sounds of wind chimes and an immense surge of relief.

There was a 'Please wait here' sign-on-a-pole in the hallway, with which I was glad to cooperate while I got my bearings and figured out what to do next. From the front room, which now seemed to function as a reception and office area, I could hear one end of a telephone conversation, from which I gathered that the practitioner was not taking any reiki appointments today as this was the occasion of a cuddle party. Except with the children, I'm not a really touchy-feely person, and cuddle parties wouldn't normally be my thing, but it's surprising what you can find yourself prepared to go along with when motivated by fear of the alternative, and I set my sights on staying in that building whatever the cost. So, when the receptionist invited me to come to her counter and asked if I was there for the cuddle party, I said I was. She took out a ledger-like book and asked my name, which I gave. She ran her finger down the page but could find no trace of me, obviously. She asked if I'd booked, because they were full for this party, and I lied that I had. She ran her finger down the names again and, still unable to find me, asked if I was sure it was this month's party for which I'd booked. Brazenly, I insisted it was.

Nevertheless, she turned to the following month's shorter list of names to see if I had been entered there. Of course, I had not. She looked at me dubiously, searching, I felt, for some clue that would give me away as an illegitimate guest. 'Did you bring your pyjamas?' she asked testily. My heart sank. I remembered hearing somewhere along the line that this was one of the cuddle-party rules – that everyone would dress in pyjamas. And then, wonder of wonders, I remembered I had Walter's new pair in my bag, bringing them home for Kathleen. I declared to the disbelieving administrator that yes – Yes! – I had my pyjamas. I was ready and prepared. (Anything rather than go out and face what was lurking in the street.)

Walter's pyjamas were a nightmare. The waistband was enormous, and they had that open-style fly that men have on their night attire. In the end, I gathered them up over one hip and tied a knot with the excess fabric. Then I threw the voluminous jacket over the top. When I started hearing other voices, mainly shrill and brittle, my anxiety returned. I mean, if you stripped away my panicked, irrational impulse, what on earth was I doing there, setting myself up for staged intimacy with strangers, all because I'd thought I heard someone behind me in the street? But someone was agitating mildly for my changing cubicle, which I had delayed leaving, and there was nothing for it but to step out and join the throng.

So, how did I get from the discomfort of gatecrashing a cuddle party to landing up in an accident and emergency ward?

The cuddling strangers provided that final twist of the screw, which promptly snapped. One minute I was in the embrace of an emaciated middle-aged woman in a lightweight Snoopy dressing-gown, my heart thumping in my chest and struggling for breath. The next I was lying groggily on the floor surrounded by a sea of slippers.

I heard a voice I recognised saying something like 'Stand back and give her some air,' and then a man in blue cotton chambray pyjamas knelt beside me and asked if I could hear him. I couldn't work my mouth properly and moaned. In the background, I could hear someone phoning for an ambulance. I thought that (a) I must be really ill, and (b) I had never been in an ambulance before.

The kneeling man, who was right over my face, smelled aggressively of shower gel. He adjusted my head and told me he was checking my airways, then pushed me on to my side and said he was putting me in the recovery position. When the ambulance came, I was loaded into a wheelchair and put into the back of the vehicle. I was shaking. I told the ambulance crew I thought I might have had a heart attack. They put an oxygen mask over my face, and I didn't try to talk any more.

I sat there trying to place the semi-familiar voice of my helper. At last, I remembered it was Neville, the first-aiding lonely heart who had failed to woo BMW-driving Pamela.

*

Of course it hadn't been a *heart* attack but a bloody *panic* attack. Tests confirmed that nothing untoward had happened to my heart in the recent past, and I was given a little lecture about hyperventilation, how quickly it can alter the blood's chemistry, how alarming and distressing it can be for the sufferer but that it's ultimately harmless. What a fool. I said I'd make arrangements to go home but was told not to rush off anywhere.

*

The reason I was told not to rush off was because another doctor was coming to see me. He was young and very nice and asked me about the not sleeping and, more recently, not eating, the phobia about rats, the isolation at work, the stress of trying to help Hugh Davy without annoying Sally Lewis, Janice, Penny, the time-and-motion study at the magazine, Terry's damning but good poems and, well, everything. It turned out the nice young doctor was a nice young psychiatrist, and he said I should come and stay in their building for about a week. I thought of how hospital wards didn't have hidey-holes for vermin and asked would he be able to give me something to make me sleep. He said he would, and I said OK.

*

Alison, the nurse, took my history. I had to stop several times to weep. Then I had to explain to Alison that, although I was weeping, it was actually making me very happy because I had previously been unable to and now I could feel it loosening the tight screw. I don't know whether it was the crying or the little yellow pill, but when I climbed into my starched bed I could feel myself, for the first time in ages, getting properly, deeply drowsy.

* * *

Slept.

* * *

Slept.

217

* * *

Could have slept quite happily, but it had been decided that I was to be got up and made to go to the dining room for meals with everyone else. It turned out I was ravenous. I shovelled down a wizened shepherd's pie with marrowfat peas and carrots, followed by a peach mousse in a plastic 'glass'. And I didn't even feel full. Maura, a kind but lethargic, motherly woman, welcomed me to the ward. Apparently her bed is next to mine. I haven't started noticing anything like that yet.

*

I was given a questionnaire thingy to pick my meal for tomorrow. I've opted for chicken-and-ham pie with mashed potatoes at lunch, then scrambled egg and toast for tea.

*

He called in to visit me after tea, alone. He wasn't sure I'd want the children seeing me 'in a place like this' (like what? It's just a hospital ward, but I suppose I know what he means). I asked him to bring them tomorrow, as well as some crisps, biscuits and something to drink. And something to read.

After he had gone, I suddenly remembered the children's packed lunches. Who is making them? Him? Eleanor? Do they know who takes butter in their sandwiches and who doesn't, and who only likes the bottom slice buttered? If their sandwiches aren't right, they'll eat nothing and collapse during afternoon lessons. I'll have to phone home. I must also nab Eleanor *re* the school jumpers. Left to his own devices, *he* will put them on with the ordinary wash and they'll go all thin and stringy.

* * *

Nurse Alison came round to my bed and told me that a 'Mark' had rung, enquiring if I was seeing visitors. I felt like the Queen. I said there were plenty of people I wouldn't want to see but Mark wasn't one of them. It would be fine if he called.

*

Maura has depression. She, too, had been unable to sleep for a protracted period before she was admitted. And she'd thought she was having heart attacks before she came into hospital, like me, through A and E. (She hadn't had heart attacks. They're sure – they put her on a machine that can tell you.) Maura's determined not to be discharged before she's better as she couldn't bear to return to what she was feeling like before she came in. She has a beautiful floral arrangement on her bedside locker as her best friend is a florist. I'd have thought you were much less likely to get into one of these states if you had a best friend to talk to, but there you go.

*

On my menu selector, I've opted for steak pie and chips followed by jelly whip at lunch, then tuna sandwiches for tea.

*

Mark brought me a copy of *Private Eye,* a box of tissues and a packet of Choco Leibniz biscuits. I felt a bit like Walter. I explained to Mark who Walter was, and he laughed. He didn't ask how I was feeling, and he didn't ask me how this had happened. He just said, 'Water in the electrics, eh?' and I said, 'Water in the electrics.' Then he told me about an Irish oak hallstand he had acquired for the shop and a leather 1930s car coat, which he had bought to sell on but to which he had now taken a real fancy. He said he was keeping an open mind on the matter of the factory-outlet park, and that while it would undoubtedly ruin the village ambience, it would also bring in a lot more consumers, so it wasn't all bad. I asked tentatively about Lindy-May, but Mark made the slightest of remarks, then changed the subject, confirming my suspicion that things are not right between her and me.

When Mark had gone, Maura asked if he was my husband. As if! I explained he was not, but I also told her that he was 'one of us' – i.e., a sufferer.

It struck me that this was the first time I had ever seen Mark when he had not been wearing his leather jacket, although he did carry it over his shoulder, with his finger through the hanging-up loop.

*

When the children came in, their light and noise was too incongruous with the gentle sorrow of the ward, so I took them, with *him*, downstairs to the former smoking room, which has a table, chairs and a vending-machine. There was space for them to run around, providing they kept in fairly small circles, and we dug up enough change for them to share a bottle of Diet Pepsi.

He has had the pest-control man in, even though he doesn't think we have anything untoward living in our house. The pest-control man agreed. He had a good look round, even climbing into the attic, where he said there wasn't so much as a mouse dropping to suggest there had ever been any wildlife about the place since it was built in 1937. He's ninety-nine per cent sure we don't have any pests of any kind on our property. Why, oh why, do I hear that as a one per cent chance that we have?

When the children, eventually, inevitably, got round to asking what was the matter with me, I said I'd been working too hard and needed a rest. That seemed sufficient. I don't wish them to look back on me, the mother of their childhood, as some kind of Sylvia Plath. Eleanor has moved into our house while I'm in hospital. Bless her. She's sleeping on the Z-bed in the littlest one's room.

Of course, with the mention of work, when I was back on the ward, my brain turned to the mall and Hilary. What explanations had been given to them, I wondered, as to my whereabouts? I confided my concerns in Nurse Alison. She said I'd only just got there, and it was supposed to be a sanctuary for me to enable me to get well. She suggested I decide what I wanted people to be told, then relay this to *him* when he visits tomorrow. This was a good plan, which left me free to read the fat novel he'd brought me, which was almost as relaxing as sleeping.

* * *

I still don't know if it's the five consecutive nights' sleep or the little yellow pill, but already I'm feeling much better and more relaxed than I have for ages. Of course, I still get the heebie-jeebies when I think of Tony and Leon knowing what I said about them permitting Penny Reynolds to steal from the mall, or when I imagine trying to break the news to Hilary that I must walk away from the search for Baby Noel's mother, or when I remember that someone hated me enough to spray 'Bitch' across my windscreen, but my strategy for the next few days is not to think about these things. Sometimes you just have to let stuff go.

Maura has started to ask me to join her when she goes outside with the smokers for their little puff. There is a greying patio table and chairs just round the corner from the front door and we're allowed to go out there to sit. They all wanted to hear about Mark, who apparently caused quite a stir walking through the ward yesterday. They wanted to know if he was my brother, which I explained he was not, and then they wanted to know if he had a girlfriend, although they're all in relationships! They want me to make sure to ask him to return so that they can ogle him a little more.

Back on the ward, Maura and I compared symptoms. Maura said no one in her family had ever had depression

222

until her, and she was so grateful that she'd never had it when her children were small, as some women do, but was fine until she hit the menopause. So, she reckons hers is the fault of her hormones. I, on the other hand, favour the genetic-predisposition scenario. As I told her, it's an open secret in our family that Terry, my father, is a chronic anxiety sufferer. When he hits one of his blips, we just call it his not being well and behave like he has a streaming head cold and must take to his bed for a fortnight. But, of course, it isn't a head cold. It's anxiety. Why don't we just say so?

*

On my menu sheet for tomorrow, I've ticked battered whiting and potatoes, followed by ginger cake and custard at lunch, bacon with bread and butter for tea.

*

I won't be able to listen to Jane Dare's matchmaker programme tonight as it's lights off at ten. I'll miss hearing about Marcella and Steve.

* * *

The smokers group is: Carol (anxiety and depression), who smokes Silk Cut; Mina (anxiety, suicidal), who smokes Embassy Regal; Cally (not sure, possibly something dark, as she dresses like a Goth) sometimes Benson & Hedges, sometimes just lights some incense; and the non-smoking participants, Maura and me. Apart from our illnesses, which we discuss at length, there is one and only one topic of conversation: shopping. For example, I now know the price, origin and quality of every item of Carol's clothing down to the shoes on her feet (£25, Matalan, fit like a glove). I know each and every garment Mina bought her granddaughter, Natalie, for going on holiday to Salou. Even Cally can hold her own in a conversation about sourcing a bargain lawnmower for a small garden, while Maura has found out where you can buy brand-name shampoo and conditioner for a fraction of the recommended retail price. At first, I thought that I had nothing to contribute to the conversation and mainly stayed quiet. But then it struck me that I had, after all, been working in nothing less than a shopping centre! So, I did like with the Country Ladies' Circle and swore them to secrecy before telling all.

*

I had a session with the nice young doctor who had admitted me. He asked how I was settling in, and I said, 'Fine.' He asked me how the food was, and I said that ever since my admission I'd had this mad appetite, which he said wasn't unusual. It might be a reaction to relief from the stress that had been building up in me, and it might also be the little yellow pill. He asked if I'd met Wilfred yet, and I said I had.

Wilfred is a little grey-haired man who looks like a fifty-year-old schoolboy. He comes and tells me when our meal is ready in the dining room and when the tea and coffee trolley arrives on the ward. Seemingly, he's equally solicitous with every new arrival. He told me he has been living on his own since his mother and father died and that he isn't coping very well. He expressed a thinly disguised interest in my bowl of oranges, and I gave him two. I wished I could do more for him, but what?

When the doctor started on the real business of our conversation, I told him my theory about inheriting my anxiety from Terry, my father. He said there is some evidence to suggest that a predisposition to anxiety may be a kind of family trait but that this includes the possibility that a child *learns* it from an anxious parent as well as the possibility that the child directly *inherits* it. I said I favoured the 'inherits' option. He said he favours the 'learns' avenue, so we'll go for a balanced approach and discuss both possibilities. He asked me if I remembered my paternal grandparents, and I said I did, vaguely. He then asked if I had been aware of them as anxious people, and I said no, I hadn't, but that I could probably check this out with my mother. He said this might be useful. I suppose it's fair enough: after all, if I'm going to claim I got my anxiety from Terry, it's not unreasonable to ask where he got his.

*

On tomorrow's menu, I've selected cottage pie with chips, then strawberry whip for lunch, and sausages, bread and butter and an apple for tea.

Is someone waking the little one and taking him for his late-night pee? I don't like to think of him in a wet bed.

* * *

Today, I was told to attend the occupational-therapy group. Maura said I could walk down with her. She's feeling pretty low. They've changed her tablets once already, even though she's only been in for ten days, and she doesn't think they gave the first tablet a chance. At occupational therapy, we did a word-search puzzle, and everybody thinks I'm 'brainy' because I got it finished in about five minutes when they'd hardly started. They don't realise that they're actually the more skilful ones, because they have the social aptitude to chat to each other instead of getting on with the task, while I can merely do as ordered.

I did manage to chip in when it came to a discussion of panic attacks. Some people's symptoms included cold hands and feet, and others said they got breathless. Maura said she nearly always got a tightness in her chest, but I was the only one who had had a falling-down faint, which seemed to earn me some kudos among my anxious peers! Because I let slip that I'd had my attack at a cuddle party, I ended up having to explain what that was as nobody but Cally had heard of them. They weren't impressed. I assured them that everyone had seemed nice and not at all the bunch of weirdos you might have expected, and that they had set aside hugging to come to my aid when I collapsed. Still, the group made all sorts of shudders and left me in no doubt that they didn't rate cuddle parties as a leisure activity. At least I'd managed to find something to talk about.

*

I've selected ham and parsley sauce with mashed potatoes for tomorrow's lunch, then egg mayonnaise and salad for tea.

I wonder what they're eating at home.

*

Tonight, *he* came in to visit me. I didn't know whether to be glad or sad that he'd left the children with Eleanor and Terry, but he brought in a get-well card that the youngest had made, depicting me with a very large head supported on a very small body, which is most insightful as it's pretty well exactly how I'd been feeling prior to admission. They'd all signed it. He also brought some cartons of juice, a packet of Twix fingers and a copy of *Hey There!*. I had to ask him to go and buy me some new pants and bring them in tomorrow as I've run out. Slightly embarrassing. I asked him about work, but he said he wasn't going to talk about that, as I was supposed to be taking time out from my worries. As if that in itself didn't let me know there must be developments worth worrying about! I told him about Wilfred and asked him to bring in a bag of oranges so that I can give them to him. He said he would.

* * *

Nothing much happens on the ward on Saturdays. There's no occupational therapy, and there are no sessions with the doctor. I lay on my bed and read *Hey There!*. There was a big speculation piece about who Lorcan Hinds was seeing – was there really something or nothing going on long-distance between him and Beth Marsh? *Hey There!,* which claimed to have spoken to an 'insider', said that if there had been anything, it was now over as Lorcan Hinds had committed himself to life in Europe for the next few months while Beth had not yet given up on Hollywood. The article said that his *Macbeth* co-stars, Francesca Annis and Billie Piper, had both been intimating privately what a pleasure it was to work with him, while he in turn had praised the professionalism and dedication of his leading ladies. So, another celebrity article that said nothing. Or almost nothing. As a footnote, it mentioned that the writers of *Mac* have turned in another brand-new feature-length script, and the producers think it's so hot that Lorcan Hinds will find it difficult to resist. A footnote! This is far more important than who the actor's girlfriend is!

*

It came up in conversation with Nurse Alison that I had missed Jane Dare's matchmaker programme on Wednesday night and was left wondering what had happened to some previous participants. Nurse Alison was able to tell me that her colleague, Nurse Pat, who does the other end of the ward, where Wilfred is, is always talking about that show, and she'd find out if Pat had heard this episode. Well, she did, and she came and sat on the edge of my bed and told me all about it. And what a tale there was to tell.

Plus-size corporate-banker Marcella and Phil Mitchell-lookalike accountant Steve had turned out to be a blinding match. Just two weeks after they'd been paired up in Jane Dare's show they'd returned triumphantly to testify that their night at Maison Philippe had been the start of a whirlwind romance, which was still gathering momentum. Within a week, Steve had stayed over at Marcella's apartment. Within ten days, they had been introduced to each other's widowed parents. By day twelve, a diamond ring had appeared, and by the time they made it to the studio, not only were they engaged to be married but Marcella's widowed mother and Steve's widowed father were seeing each other, too. Wow!

I had a little twinge when I thought how I normally listen to the radio quietly in bed because the children are sleeping just down the corridor, but no doubt I'll be home soon, so I tried not to dwell on this.

*

For tomorrow's lunch, I've ordered roast beef and roast potatoes followed by baked rice pudding. For tea, I've requested vegetable soup followed by shortbread.

* * *

Today, Eleanor came to see me and brought me a new seven-pack of supermarket pants with some sanitary towels in case I needed them, which I did not. She asked me how I was, and I said I was feeling much better. She asked me what the food was like, and I said not bad. In fact, by objective standards, it is probably pretty bad, but I'm so hungry that I don't seem to care. It was the first time Eleanor had seen me since my admission, and I felt she wanted to ask how I'd ended up there but was afraid of saying the wrong thing, so I explained to her some of what had been on my mind just before I flipped out. She seemed to take it all in.

It then occurred to me that she must be wondering what the hell I'd been doing at a cuddle party in the first place, and in a pair of outsize men's pyjamas, so I explained that one, too, noting as I spoke that the stuff about someone following me sounded like textbook paranoia. 'I'm not paranoid,' I insisted. And I told her about the cream graffiti on the windscreen. For some reason, I started to laugh about it, a bit madly, just laughing, laughing so I could hardly get the words out, and then I began to sob, and you'd think I'd be cried out by now, but I wasn't.

Nurse Pat noticed from the workstation at the centre of the ward and did a little stroll past. She asked me if everything was all right and glanced at Eleanor, as if to say, 'Is she upsetting you?' I managed to stop crying and say I was fine, just a few tears.

When I'd settled down and Eleanor was about to leave, I remembered I had to ask her about my paternal grandparents and whether they'd been anxious. Eleanor thought for a moment, then told me that my grandmother was probably best described as 'feisty', before being feisty became fashionable, while my grandfather was overwhelmingly gentle, which was also quite distinctive in a man of his generation. But she wouldn't have thought of either of them as anxious, no. She also told me she was fine on the Z-bed and didn't want me hurrying home until I was properly fixed.

* * *

In the middle of the night, a woman was brought in noisily. She was pleading with the nurses not to make her take a tablet, and they were being very no-nonsense, telling her she had to take it and it would make her feel better. Everybody in the ward must have heard the commotion, but nobody stirred. Did we really choose to mind our own business because this was the right thing to do, or have we just become institutionalised?

*

For occupational therapy today, we had a quiz, with mixed-sex teams. Guess who was on my team, along with Maura and Wilfred? The elderly schoolmaster from Walter's nursing-home who can remember everything brilliantly until the 1970s, then very little. He has been here for several weeks being treated for depression and is now almost perky and nearly ready to return to the home. He said he's in no rush as he finds the atmosphere in the psychiatric building a lot more stimulating than it is in the other place. He and I answered most of the questions between us, with a little help from Maura, who knew the cookery answers and also Torville and Dean's first names.

Wilfred didn't appear to know anything whatsoever on any subject, and it's hard to understand what sort of life he must have lived to avoid so completely picking up any passing knowledge of anything at all in his fifty-odd years.

Our team won the prize, which was a bag of liquorice allsorts each. I don't like liquorice, so I gave mine to Wilfred, who seemed a hundred per cent pleased with the deal and not even one per cent disappointed on my behalf that I came away with nothing. Like a small child.

*

Maura had to fill in my menu sheet for me as I was away having a shower. Because of her medication, she cannot remember what she ticked. She was most apologetic. I told her it didn't matter. It would be like a lucky dip. And it won't matter, as long as she didn't tick anything with liver or mushrooms.

*

The noisy woman who was admitted at night seems to be in the sideward by the nurses' workstation. They take it in shifts to sit in her doorway filling in their paperwork.

* * *

I fell asleep on top of my bed, and when I woke up, who was sitting in my bedside chair with her unshod feet up on the bed frame, flipping through my *Hey There!* magazine and eating one of my oranges but Lindy-May. I was totally surprised to see her. When she saw I was awake, she said,

'Well, sleepyhead,' like there was nothing wrong between us and never had been, which sent me into confusion all over again. I'd been so sure I'd offended her somehow and that she was giving me the cold shoulder. (I'd never seriously suspected her of the cream graffiti, but on the other hand I hadn't ruled her out.) And now there she sat.

Before we could get talking, Nurse Pat came past, looking for Wilfred to fill in his menu selection. She paused with me and Lindy-May, and at first I thought perhaps Pat had recognised her, but then Pat said, to Lindy-May, not to me, 'Are you feeling all right? Would you like a cup of tea and a piece of toast?'

This struck me as a rather strange offer to a hospital visitor, and I expected Lindy-May to find it strange, too, but she just said that would be great. Then Pat said, conspiratorially, 'I'm right, aren't I?' giving a little nod towards Lindy-May, who smiled wearily, I thought, and conceded that, yes, Pat was right.

Right about what? What on earth were they talking about? What was there to notice about Lindy-May today, except that her spiky silver hair was a little oily, and she was wearing her shirt out over her skirt in a way that she didn't usually? It wasn't that I wanted to be the centre of attention, exactly, but what could this nurse and this visitor possibly have in common to talk about but me? So, I asked Lindy-May, 'Right about what?' And she said, 'Right about me being pregnant.'

I didn't know what to say. Was this an occasion for congratulation or commiseration? Lindy-May had never given any hints one way or the other about whether or not she would have liked children. For all I knew she could be thrilled or devastated. And should I assume that Harry Ferris was the father? Or might that be another howler? I was afraid to utter a sound in case I put my big foot into my mouth.

'That's shut you up,' observed Lindy-May, correctly.

So I came out and told her I didn't know what to say as I didn't know how she felt about the situation. She replied, 'Well, put it like this. I wasn't planning on becoming a first-time mother at the age of forty-four, but now that it's happening I'm going to take things as they come. And, yes, it's Harry's. And, no, he's not going to leave his wife, and I don't want him to.' She wasn't sure how long she wanted to take off work, but she did know that she'd be looking for a nanny, preferably a well-upholstered middle-aged one who wouldn't distract the father when he was visiting.

All that time I had thought Lindy-May was being a bit distant with me, she was actually agonising over the possibility, then the certainty that she was pregnant. And all that time I'd thought she was avoiding me, she'd actually been avoiding the food smells of the canteen, because of all-day morning sickness. She'd told me that day in the lift, months ago, that if she ever fell out with me I'd be left in no doubt about it – well, I'd thought this had been it.

Eventually, after Lindy-May had filled in my menu sheet for tomorrow (lasagne with green salad and ice cream for lunch, beef stew and a banana for tea), we had talked about how well Mark seemed, these days, and I had passed on the summary of Jane Dare's most recent wildly successful match-making, she asked me how I had ended up in the psychiatric building when there didn't appear to be anything wrong with me.

I admitted that I felt much better than I had at the time of my admission and tried to explain that a lot of stresses had been building up in me, to which I had reacted by becoming very anxious and, as far as I knew, the only reason my anxiety had started to abate was because I was currently hiding from everything in hospital. Lindy-May said that Mark was like me, even though he was well at the moment. I said I knew. Lindy-May said she didn't really understand, as she didn't get anxious about anything. I said she was lucky and that I didn't want to tempt Fate but to get back to me on that one when she'd had her baby for six months.

After her tea and toast, she stayed for a little longer. I asked who knew about the pregnancy, and she said probably most people by now, as she'd felt she had to tell Hilary, her producer, and Hilary wasn't renowned for keeping things to herself. I asked what would happen about the Baby Noel project now that I was incapacitated, and Lindy-May rolled her eyes. I was definitely not to worry about that one. She said Hilary had come up with this people-tracing pilot idea totally on her own, and no one else at the station thought it was a good one, and if it fell by the wayside, nobody could care less except Hilary, who wasn't as important as she liked to think. The only thing was, I might not get paid even for the work I'd already done.

Wilfred came by. Seeing Lindy-May lifting her handbag, he asked her if she had any sweets. She dug out most of a packet of barley sugar, which she'd been sucking for her morning sickness, and gave it to him, calling him 'sweetheart'. Wilfred beamed like a little boy, took the sweets and went away. Lindy-May gave me a look that seemed to question whether I belonged in the same place as the child-man. Then she leaned over me, smoothed my hair off my face, said she'd see me soon, and she was gone.

Maura asked whether my visitor had been Lindy-May from Zero FM, and I said yes. I could see she was impressed.

*

In the middle of the evening, the distressed woman in the sideward became distressed again and started shouting, but I think the nurses gave her something very quickly because she'd hardly begun when it all returned to quiet.

* * *

I saw my young psychiatrist again, today. He has put two and two together and made four – i.e., he has worked out that I'm the daughter of Terry, the quite famous poet. (We do have rather an unusual surname.) He could see me recoil at this revelation and assured me that the connection would not affect the course of my treatment, but I'm not convinced: if he likes Terry's poetry, surely he'll harbour a certain bias in his favour. Already he's bringing the poems into the conversation, and I don't see what they have to do with me learning not to react to everything by getting anxious, although the doctor insists this is exactly what he's pursuing.

*

Even I could see that today's lasagne had been baked to a frazzle while the beef stew seemed to have been made by trimming the fat off the meat, then putting the fat and not the other part in. My appetite must be evening out.

*

Maura's grown-up daughter came in this evening. She brought magazines and fruit salad. I saw that she was wearing a pair of 'Carnival' sandals.

If he doesn't bring in our children soon, they'll start to forget me.

* * *

Cally, the Goth girl, and I got talking this morning during the smokers' break-time. She's here because she scared the wits out of herself with a ouija board. She'd wanted to be a white witch but is now too frightened of the power of magic. She also knows Michelle, the other store detective from the mall, as they attended the shero workshops together.

*

Kathleen and Lorna came in to see me today. They brought me some Robinson's Orange Barley Water, a Tupperware box of Kathleen's home-made shortbread and a tabloid newspaper. (They're seasoned hospital visitors.) It had been spinning through my head all morning that I'd been supposed to ask round the Riverside mall for tombola prizes for our school summer fête, and I hadn't. Kathleen and Lorna are often in the mall in a normal week, so I braved it and asked if they'd take over this mission and, thank goodness, they said yes.

*

Either the food is getting worse or my tastes have reverted to normal. Slimy bacon, waxy boiled potatoes and mushy cabbage, followed by a trifle with no custard. That's not a trifle!

*

Nurse Pat came and sat on my bed for a while and updated me on the Jane Dare matchmaking feature. Apparently last night's lonely heart was a retired lady called Bella who works in a charity shop three mornings a week, lives alone with her poodle but sees a lot of her son and daughter-in-law and their family, whose weekly ironing she always does and fetches round to them in her Suzuki Swift with power-steering. Nurse Pat said Bella sounded a bit well-to-do. She got her three return calls, but they were all hopeless and had nothing to say for themselves. Bella eventually picked William, who was possibly the least reticent, and who was widowed and had recently handed the reins of his double-glazing business to his children, so he sounded as if he had plenty of time and money.

Then she got me talking a bit about other radio shows I listen to, and which TV shows I watch (she, too, is mad about Lorcan Hinds) and what I had been doing as a job, and how long she'd been working here, and what friendships I had.

Some people might think this was idle chit-chat, but I've been talked to like this by a therapist before, and what they do is they remember your answers and go off round the corner to write it all down. So, it didn't make me cagey, exactly, but let's just say I knew what was going on.

* * *

Kathleen and Lorna were back this afternoon to show me the prizes they'd solicited for the summer fête tombola. Nursery World had given them a baby bath-book and a child's cutlery set featuring Paddington Bear. Pharmacity had donated a set of make-up brushes and a jar of unisex hair gel. Diggers Discount Jewellery had presented them with a suedette jewellery roll. The juice bar had pressed on them a carton of black drinking straws. The discount designer place had given half a dozen of their own-brand calico shopping-bags. The young women's fashion place had handed over a cheap-looking belt. From the stationer's/ wannabe bookshop, they'd got a lilac stationery set and a boxed plastic desk tidy, while the supermarket had come up trumps with two pairs of tights, two pairs of men's socks, two water-pistols and two skipping-ropes. Then, when they bumped into Moira Reynolds and she heard what they were doing, she pushed four of the mall's goodie bags – little nylon gym bags with pencils, rubbers, rollerball pens and light-up keyrings, all bearing the mall logo – into their hands. Kathleen and Lorna are absolute stars. All the smokers, plus Maura, gathered round for a nosy, and now they're planning to be out in time to come to our summer fête because they think it sounds really good and they want to meet Harry Ferris.

*

My doctor popped on to the ward to see me before he went home. I was doing the quiz word in *Hey There!*, but I dare say he's seen worse. He set something down on my wheeled table. I couldn't believe what it was: a copy of my father's first volume of poetry. At first, I thought he was going to ask me to get it signed, but this was not his purpose. He said he wanted me to read 'Girl on a Gate'. That old thing! Bad enough to have to read your own father's poems for your A-level exam but to be asked to do the same in your middle years when you've landed yourself in hospital! I could have told him I didn't need the book: I know every line. But I was so taken aback by his request – if it was a request, perhaps it was more of a prescription – and am so naturally inclined to do as I'm told that I agreed. Read 'Girl on a Gate', indeed.

* * *

Moira Reynolds came to see me today. She has alternate Saturdays off with Ted Twome. She brought me a basket of fruit with a red bow on it and a get-well-soon card signed by absolutely loads of names from work. I looked to see if Tony and Leon's were present, and they were. She also brought me a get-well card from the Country Ladies' Circle, signed as a collective, presumably by Eileen Brogan.

Apparently, Eileen had called into the mall to see me. The local Circle had been asked to provide a guest speaker for their district convention in October, and her committee had unanimously agreed that I was the woman for the job. Eileen had asked Moira if she thought I'd be willing to repeat my 'turn', and Moira had explained that I was ill, without saying with what, but had agreed to raise the matter with me. I'm quite chuffed but daunted too. Also, I don't want to count my chickens about being properly well again – although I can't see this blip lasting till the autumn – and I'm still afflicted with the most popular phobia, which is of public speaking.

As I feared she might, Moira raised the subject of the last conversation I'd had with her before my flip-out. This was when I'd told her about her daughter Penny thieving with impunity from the Riverside mall, although I'd left out the rather major detail of the thief's identity. Moira said she'd thought a lot about what I'd said, regarding tolerance of this person's activities by other members of staff, and had

241

decided to do nothing for now. She said Tony and Leon were excellent at their jobs, and there hadn't been the slightest suggestion from any other quarter that they were less than professional, so she was going to give them the benefit of the doubt. She said they had worked at the mall satisfactorily for several years while I had been there a matter of months, so she had to put her faith in them, which didn't mean she didn't have faith in me, but we'd just put it down to my being stressed at the time, and I wasn't to be offended. Offended? No way! She'd said basically that we were going to forget the matter. I was relieved.

She asked if I'd heard Lindy-May's news. I said I had. Moira looked as if she required me to make some sort of comment, but I didn't want to. Lindy-May has been good to me, so I said nothing. Apparently, Penny Reynolds has given Lindy-May some peppermint balm to rub on her temples, and it's done wonders for her morning sickness. Probably stolen property.

*

I read 'Girl on a Gate' again. Same old same old. I mean, I know it's good. It's clever the way the rhythm of the words describes the swinging action of the gate, in and out, and the rhymes emphasise the pattern, too. And I understand that the garden imagery is supposed to suggest the Garden of Eden and the innocence that that implies. I do get it. I just don't get what a forty-year-old poem about a girl swinging

242

on a gate has to do with me being riddled with anxiety in the here and now.

* * *

It seems that the hospital kitchen does a roast dinner every Sunday. Today, it was stuffed pork with carrots, peas and roast potatoes. Actually, it wasn't bad.

*

This afternoon, Mark came to see me. He brought a book of after-dinner humour from Brian and Sheelagh and a bunch of flowers from himself. Nurse Alison and the two ward assistants were practically elbowing each other out of the way for the privilege of taking the flowers and putting them into a vase. Mark seems to have this effect on women. During his visit, most of the smokers' circle drifted by as if to say hi but really to get a closer, better look at him.

The mechanical diggers have moved into the village where Mark has his shop. They've started gouging out the foundations for the factory-outlet park. Mark says there's no point fighting, it and he might as well hope for an upturn in passing trade.

Wilfred came along while he was there. He stood very still for a minute then announced that the tea trolley would soon be up. But, really, he was giving Mark the evil eye, recognising that this was not the man who had brought him the bag of oranges – a man to whom he had therefore forged a kind of loyalty. When Wilfred had gone, Mark asked, 'Did

I do something wrong?', and I told him he hadn't brought any oranges, and Mark said, 'Ah.' And I bet the next time he comes he brings oranges for Wilfred.

I reported to Mark that my doctor had told me to read 'Girl on a Gate' and that I was dubious about this having any part in my treatment. Mark seemed to consider the matter seriously, then said he thought that the doctor must mean me to read it not so much as a poem but as something that had happened to Terry and might have affected him. I hadn't wanted him to make any such suggestion. I had simply wanted him to agree with me about the ridiculousness of the request, so I mentally filed his comment under 'Yeah, yeah.'

I noticed that Mark sat on my bedside chair for the duration of the visit while his leather jacket lay on the foot of my bed.

When Mark had gone, I was able to report to the smokers'/shoppers' circle that work has commenced on the new factory-outlet park. It was immediately clear that I had said the right thing, and we got a good half an hour's conversation out of discussing which factory outlets were rumoured to be coming to the project, plus the relative merits of other factory outlets we had been to (none, in my case).

*

What exactly did Mark mean, read it as something that had happened to Terry and might have affected him?

* * *

Something has happened on the ward. That is, it happened days ago but I just went on eating my big hospital dinners and swanning about with Maura and the smokers totally unaware of what had taken place. The distressed woman in the sideward has a name. And her name is Sally Lewis. I found this out while I was waiting at the nurses' workstation for the key to the shower room. I overheard them talking about her.

I want to hide under my bed. I want to be transferred to another ward. I just know that Sally Lewis would never have been under constant watch in a sideward were it not for me pushing and prodding her about Baby Noel. And if I feel like this about her being here, how is she going to feel when she eventually emerges from the sideward and finds me?

*

I filled in my menu sheet with chilli and rice, followed by blancmange, for tomorrow's lunch, then a jumbo chicken vol-au-vent and a peach for tea, but I can't imagine eating any of it.

* * *

At occupational therapy this morning (which was realio trulio basket-weaving, can you believe it?), I was so subdued that everybody was asking me what was wrong. I explained I'd discovered that I knew the woman in the sideward, and Cally said, 'Oh, you mean the one on suicide watch?' And I probably should have worked this out from the constant nursing vigil, but actually I hadn't, so I felt worse and blurted out that I suspected I had quite a lot to do with the state she was in. Nobody believed me because I've created the impression that I'm basically harmless. I couldn't tell them the story, because that would have been unfair to Sally Lewis, who is presumably going to come out from that sideward one of these days and doesn't need to find that the tale of Baby Noel has preceded her. So, I had to sit on my worries as on a nestful of eggs waiting to hatch.

*

This evening, Michelle, the afternoon store detective, came to see me. She brought me the new *Hey There!* and an energy drink. She wanted to tell me that, since she's done her exams at the end of her university access course, she's now available to work full-time and that Moira has offered her my shifts at the mall as well as her usual afternoons, but she's happy to step aside as soon as I'm well enough to return.

I said her new hours were safe for the foreseeable future. She asked if anyone had told me that the civil-servant shoplifter (whose name, it turns out, is Alice Lacey) has written to Ted Twome admitting the shoplifting, apologising for it and for her behaviour afterwards and offering to pay for the goods she tried to take!

I, in turn, told Michelle about the UHT cream graffiti on my car windscreen and, after discussion, we agreed that it was unlikely to be the civil-servant shoplifter, who had clearly been under solicitor's orders to make peace.

Then Michelle had a brilliant idea. She said, 'I know your car. It's the big old estate with a scratch over the petrol flap, isn't it?' It was – is. 'And you always park it in the same spot, don't you?' she asked, and apart from the ill-fated day of the cuddle party, I do.

Well, Michelle didn't know that I always park in the space with the most room to swing a big long car to extricate it: she thought I always parked there because it was right under the CCTV camera! So, now she's rushing back to the mall where she's going to check the tapes and see if there's still a recording of the day my car was sprayed with cream. (On the one hand, I don't want to know for sure the identity of someone who hates me enough to do it. On the other, I want to be able to rule out all the people who might have done it but didn't.)

After Michelle had gone, I tried to read my new magazine but couldn't concentrate. I tried to think of 'Girl on a Gate' as an event in Terry's life but couldn't get past the poetry. Because all I can really think of is Sally Lewis. When he was admitting me, the doctor had invited me to come in for about a week. It's way over that now. Is there a chance I could be released before Sally comes out of her sideward?

* * *

Terry came to see me. He's finished his first phase of writing and is now giving himself a month's break before he starts revisions. Although I didn't want to dampen his enthusiasm for his work, I thought of him all free and giddy, and I thought of Eleanor saving my bacon by looking after the children and trying to get a decent night's sleep on a Z-bed, and I told him I thought the poems were unkind to her.

He was shocked. He asked me which ones I meant. I said most of them, but especially the one where he laments a life spent not looking at the stars because of being so busy looking down, trying to avoid treading in poo on the pavement.

Then we tried to move on and talk about other things, but the problem with the poems hung in the air between us and wouldn't go away.

Eventually, my father said he wouldn't hurt my mother for the world and that he'd look at the poems again as soon as he got home. He thanked me for pointing out what I had, but when he slunk off, we were both heavy of heart.

*

Because Terry was fresh in my mind, I lay on my bed and read 'Girl on a Gate' again, and the strangest thing happened. It was as though I had seen it for the first time. Out through the rhythm and rhyme climbed the familiar story, but for the first time ever I found myself thinking, But what happens after the poem ends? I'm sure that this was what the doctor was getting at, and what Mark sees. This was the key. I can hardly wait to share my new thoughts with my young doctor.

* * *

Sally Lewis has been moved out of her sideward and into a bed facing Maura. She hasn't recognised me yet, and I've been keeping the curtains pulled round my bed more than usual until I know what to do. I may consult Nurse Alison.

*

Food not good. Bright pink sausages and grey mash followed by sticky semolina.

*

When the shop trolley came round, I popped out from behind my curtains and bought a tabloid with the headline 'Beth Preggers.' It is about Beth Marsh being with child. Obviously, the speculation is that the father is Lorcan Hinds.

*

Kathleen and Lorna came in. Kathleen was wearing a sleeveless blouse and no tights as she's trying to acclimatise her skin to the sun before France. Lorna was in great form as she's just had a new battery fitted in her hearing-aid and now doesn't miss every third word like she used to do. They brought me grapes, which Kathleen had washed then dried with kitchen roll, and a bag of butterscotch. I think they found it a bit claustrophobic having the curtains pulled round the bed. It limited their ability to glance round for things to talk about. They didn't stay long.

*

Nurse Alison said she'd have a word with Sally Lewis about

my presence on the ward. She didn't see it having to be a problem as we were both in the same boat, now.

*

On my way back up from the smokers' outside chat, I saw my doctor hurrying through the ward. I rushed over to ask him if it was possible to talk about 'Girl on a Gate' today. He said no, but he'd try to see me tomorrow.

*

When *he* came in at late visiting (bearing two more fat novels and a pile of clean pants), I told him about reading Terry's old poem and understanding for the first time that it held a momentous event in Terry's development, which might explain why he is as he is. Unfortunately, *he* doesn't do poetry, so the conversation didn't go anywhere, but I can hardly wait to talk to my insightful doctor.

* * *

After breakfast, Nurse Alison came and sat on my bed and explained that it wasn't ward policy to keep the curtains pulled during the day. I reminded her about the Sally Lewis situation which, it turned out, she hadn't forgotten. In fact, she'd decided to take me across and introduce me to Sally, so we could get things out into the open. I'd rather have continued hiding, but at least Nurse Alison would be there to help.

Sally Lewis was wearing the same cardigan and slippers I had seen on her in her front room. She was docile, in a medicated sort of way, but she remembered me clearly. I said I was truly sorry if I'd played any part in her ending up in hospital. She didn't say I had, but she didn't say I hadn't. Then she asked, 'Are you still in touch with that lad?'

She could only have meant Hugh Davy. I said I'd been on the ward for a couple of weeks now, but that I knew how to get in touch with him if she had any information. Nurse Alison said Sally didn't need to worry about it now – she could see to things when she was better. Sally Lewis seemed to accept this. Remembering that she was a smoker, I told her that some of us went outside from time to time for a puff and a chat. I said I'd let her know when we were going and she'd be welcome to join us. She wasn't sure.

*

Later in the morning Mark, strolled through our ward. He didn't stop with me, though, but blew me a kiss and kept going. He was carrying a plastic carrier-bag, which was swinging weightily and filled, I'll wager, with oranges.

*

When is my young doctor coming by? I urgently wish to talk to him.

*

This morning, I didn't want to go to occupational therapy, in case I missed the doctor being on the ward, but Nurse Alison promised she'd mention it to him if he showed and made me go anyway. Once I was there, I had a strange conversation

251

with the dementia-suffering ex-schoolmaster. That is, he did the talking. I watched and listened.

It started when he saw Sally Lewis sitting at the next table. He said quietly, 'That one's been a long time coming.' I wanted to know what he meant but without actually having to ask him. I was in luck.

He said, 'Do you see that girl?' by which he meant, Do you see Sally Lewis?, who's sixty if she's a day.

I said I did.

He said, 'That girl has been sitting on a secret for thirty years.'

I said, 'Really?'

He said, 'Yes. And there's always a price to pay for that sort of thing. It's a wonder she didn't end up in here years ago.'

And then he wondered whether the doctors and nurses knew about Sally keeping a secret and wondered how they could help her if they didn't know. And he wasn't a man to break a confidence, he said, and he hadn't said a word about it for thirty years, but the girl was clearly in a bad way, and how did you decide what was for the best? He went over and spoke to Sally Lewis. I couldn't hear what they were saying, but I got the impression that he was trying to get her to look him in the eye, and she wouldn't.

*

My doctor never came. Seemingly, he was doing out-patients all morning, and then discharging people who were going

252

home for the weekend, and then he got called to another admission through A and E.

Nurse Alison had asked me if I wanted to go home for the weekend, but I declined. Of course I'd love to have time with the children, but when I think about going out I still get panicky, so I don't think I'm quite there yet.

* * *

Radio-date couple Marcella and Steve and their courting parents have become local celebrities. They've been over to London to do daytime television – not that we see it in here, but Nurse Pat knows all the gossip – and they're going to be the VIPs at the county agricultural show, held in the village where Mark has his shop.

*

There are no little chats with our doctors at the weekends, so I'll have to hold on to my discovery until Monday.

*

The ward assistant brought us a DVD of the film *Millions* to watch in the residents' lounge. People talked through it a bit, which normally I cannot abide, but perhaps I'm growing more tolerant. Sally Lewis didn't talk through it. She didn't speak at all. Carol, the smoker, fancies the actor James Nesbitt. Maura said her son looks a bit like James Nesbitt but with more hair.

* * *

Hurray! The children came to see me today, bearing gifts. The eldest brought me a bottle of orange crush, the middle one brought a terracotta crocodile he'd made in art, and the youngest one brought me a packet of Starburst, which he urgently needed me to open and share. Maura said hello to them and smiled. They said hello back, and the smallest one shook her hand. Their father, who looked tired, dropped the latest *Hey There!* onto my bed and fell into the visitors' chair. Wilfred shuffled up the corridor and regarded our family tableau silently for a few minutes before saying, 'The teas'll soon be ready.' I thanked him and offered him a Starburst. He took two but had the good grace to look sheepish.

* * *

At last, my meeting with my young doctor. 'Girl on a Gate' goes like this: a young boy comes home from school every day at the same time and is greeted every day by the little girl next door, swinging in and out on her gate, pink ribbons in her blonde hair, saying his name in her baby voice, giggling at him and putting up her face for a kiss. It's a little love story of the kind that can happen between an older child and a younger one, entirely devoid of any sinister undertones and altogether sweetly endearing. But then, one day, a terrible thing happens. The boy comes home from school, and there is no swinging gate, no little blonde girl, no kiss. There is merely silence. This is because the little girl had left her perch some time earlier, strayed out onto the road and been killed by a car. This is the fact, but nobody talks to the poet about it. When the tiny coffin is taken from the house, he ventures out to watch and swings on his own gate, for which he gets a backhander from a passer-by for being disrespectful. End of poem. My poor father.

The young doctor thinks this experience must have given my father a sense of the world as a dangerous place, a place where annihilation could occur without warning, without explanation and without acknowledgement. No wonder he grew up anxious. And it hadn't happened to me. I hadn't had anyone dear to me snatched when I was a child, but I lived as though I had because I had copied Terry's anxious habits.

So now I know. I guess the next step is working out how to undo my anxious ways, but that's not a matter for today. Today, it's enough to know what I now know.

* * *

Marilyn Softly and Miss Morning came in to see me full of excitement. Miss Morning could hardly wait to tell me that Marilyn has been approached by a leading catalogue company to model for them, after she appeared in the eco-friendly brochure in the Cornwall shots. Marilyn has folded up her market stall and is going to sell her leftover stock at a car-boot sale. What she can't shift, she'll give to one of the charity shops.

Wilfred came over and stood silently near us. Marilyn gave him a funny look, but Miss Morning smiled and said hello. I introduced him, and Miss Morning took a bag of chocolate toffee rolls out of her handbag and offered them to him first. Wilfred stepped up and, to his immense credit, took only one. Miss Morning must have made quite an impression.

*

When *he* came in to visit me in the evening, I asked him if tomorrow he'll bring in our little black phone book. I want to have access to Hugh Davy's telephone number.

*

A get-well card came from Woods and Wendy. How did they hear about me? And what did they hear? I wonder what people are saying.

The children are being splendid. While this is almost completely what I want, and I certainly don't wish any of them to cry themselves to sleep over my absence, shouldn't they be acting out their abandonment anxieties in some small way?

*

Imagine that all these years of becoming anxious around flying, lifts, going over bridges, going under bridges, multi-storey car parks, enclosed spaces generally, travelling in particularly insubstantial cars, graveyards, hospital dramas, mice and rats, etc., etc., can be traced back to what happened with the little girl on the gate. I mean, not all of it, obviously – not even the young psychiatrist was saying there were no other factors. But being raised by an anxious parent is a pretty good recipe for anxiety in the child. If only the little girl had stayed on her gate that day, not been struck, not died, how different our lives might have been.

* * *

Sally Lewis summoned me across the ward this morning. She asked me straight out if I could get Hugh Davy to come and see her. I said I didn't know but I could try, though maybe we should ask Nurse Alison first. So then we got Nurse Alison over and she tried to get her head round why Sally Lewis should be asking some man from Wales who was looking for his birth family to visit her in hospital, and she said she'd ask the doctor about it when he came on the ward. You see, once you're in hospital, it's a matter of doing what you're allowed to do.

It was time to go to occupational therapy then, but Sally wouldn't go. She's looking very grey.

We made flowers out of tissue paper. Why? Wilfred's was orange and purple and wouldn't sit up like the rest. He gave it to the occupational therapist. There's no way of knowing whether it was a tribute because he really likes her or because it was crap and he didn't want it.

*

When the doctor came round – not my young doctor but a different, older man – he called me into a side room to talk about the Sally Lewis situation. Nobody had previously told him anything about Hugh Davy's search or Sally's part in it.

He asked me why I thought she wanted to speak to him now. I said there was some feeling that she'd known his mother from the start and had been hiding her identity to protect her – she was, perhaps, a younger family member who'd had to keep her pregnancy secret. I thought it might be that Sally could no longer bear the weight of staying quiet, particularly now that she'd seen Hugh again, grown-up and face to face. The doctor listened to me but didn't tell me what he intended to do about it. Why should he?

A little later, he went and sat down beside Sally, who was lying on her bed looking at the ceiling tiles. He pulled the curtains round them for privacy then proceeded to talk in a voice that, though soft, was perfectly audible to Maura and me. We exchanged a look. He said he wasn't going to advise Sally what to do with the information she'd been carrying – if any – for these thirty years, but the staff on the ward would support her in whatever she chose to do.

In the evening, Sally's posse came round. I found myself staring at them, trying to figure out if one was the right age to be Hugh Davy's mother. At one point, Sally went for a little walk aided by a quiet, dark-haired woman of about fifty, and I wondered if this was it, if the dark-haired woman was even now being told that Sally was going to come out to Hugh Davy with the truth, but who knows?

* * *

I've done it. At Sally Lewis's request, I've phoned Hugh Davy in Wales and asked him to come and visit her in hospital as she wishes to talk to him. He will be here on Saturday.

*

I'm starting to feel so hyped now about my 'Girl on a Gate' discovery, plus the Sally Lewis development, that filling in my menu sheet seems such a trivial distraction.

*

My young doctor came round again, and we went into the little room where we go for a chat. We've agreed that I should be referred for cognitive behavioural therapy to try to retrain my responses so that I don't always react with anxiety. He said it might help with my perfectionism too, which he said would probably have crept into my job at the Riverside mall if I'd stayed there long enough. I asked whether Terry should be referred for therapy, but the young doctor explained that he wasn't his patient and also pointed out that, however Terry responded to conditions, he hadn't landed up in hospital via A and E. Unlike me. I took the point.

* * *

Sally Lewis looks grim. Surely the nurses should be giving her something. She seems racked with pain. They make her go to the canteen, but she doesn't eat anything. How will she find the strength to get through tomorrow's encounter with Hugh?

*

This afternoon, the dark-haired woman was back on her own to see Sally. They went shuffling off for the longest time. Much longer than it takes to smoke two or even three cigarettes. And when Sally returned, she was alone. She could hardly make it to the bed. I went to support her the last few steps, and I think she was on the verge of collapse.

*

This evening, Kathleen and Lorna came in. They brought me a bunch of pink and yellow carnations and *Hey There!*. They're still preparing for France. They've each bought themselves a wheeled suitcase so they can be sure to manage their own luggage as Simon will have his hands full with the children and the family bags. They asked how I was getting on, and whether I thought I'd be home soon. I told them a little bit about Terry and the learned anxiety, and they were shocked. They'd always thought Terry was a scream, and I thought, Yes, but after you've all gone, he's still screaming – on the inside. Do I tell Terry what the young doctor and I think, or do I keep it to myself? Would the news crush or enlighten him? Or both?

*

It is exactly one week until the school summer fête. Will I be out in time to attend?

* * *

Sometimes you hear a line and it's so apt, or so pithy, or so completely balanced that you instantly feel the poetry of it.

Like 'Jesus wept' or 'I am dying, Egypt, dying.' You don't actively try to learn it, you just can't forget it. I can't forget what Sally Lewis said this afternoon when Hugh Davy turned up.

Maura, the smokers and I had stuck rather closer than usual to the ward, going out for fewer and swifter puffs than usual and not even getting into any retail talk. And we knew why: the gossip was doing the rounds about Sally, Sally's younger sister – the dark-haired woman – and Baby Noel. Everybody wanted to be on hand to see what unfolded. We weren't disappointed.

When afternoon visiting came, we hardly bothered with our own families – we had our eyes and ears on stalks for Hugh. This time, he had travelled with his wife, Jenny, who accompanied him to the ward where a hush greeted them. And, out of the hush, came something like a dog howling, then Sally Lewis flew from her seat, clasping her throat, and threw herself at Hugh Davy. I will never forget the sound of her voice or the words she cried – and it was a cry from the heart, I'm sure: 'I HAVE HUNGERED FOR YOU!' And her voice dissolved into big sobs.

Hugh Davy put his arms round her, and his wife Jenny sat down mildly on the edge of Sally's bed, and we found out that Sally Lewis's sister had not been Baby Noel's mother, and neither had it been a young stranger from the seaside town. It had been Sally herself, and she'd kept the secret because she was a married woman at that time and the baby's father was someone he shouldn't have been. In those days, that was reason enough to hand over your little child, never to see him again.

Nurse Alison wasn't working, but Nurse Jackie, who does weekends, came and asked Sally, Hugh and Jenny if they'd like to use one of the interview rooms, which they did. I don't think anyone begrudged them their privacy after witnessing a moment like that. And you could tell, when they'd gone, that people felt the urge to discuss the revelation, yet nobody did. We seemed to remember we had families of our own to talk to and did that instead.

My lot came in a little late. Their dad had taken them to Trevor and Jill's shop to buy sports sandals for the summer. *He* said it had been a nightmare, and he was a bit grey. I could have told him. Apparently, the eldest had lain down on the floor of the shop, complaining of being tired, the youngest had danced on the electronic foot-measurer, which has a big sign on it, saying, 'I'm not a toy. Please do not let children play on me', and the middle one had suddenly refused to have anything to do with sandals on the grounds that they were 'gay'.

He said that at that moment he thoroughly regretted their liberal upbringing and would have loved to give them three good smacks. Each. Instead, he has threatened that if they don't behave really well for the next week, they will not be going to the summer fête. They've responded to this with a sulky silence. It didn't bother me, as I knew I only had to put up with it for forty-five minutes of visiting. But I reckon

I'm in a similar position to them: if I behave well for the next week, I might be at the fête, too.

* * *

High-fiving Michelle came to see me with some news. In her own time, she's been checking the CCTV footage of my car in the car park on the day it was creamed. She has pinpointed the culprit. It was not Alice Lacey, the civil-servant shoplifter. It was a small blonde woman of about thirty who is unknown to Michelle. She says it must be somebody I know and she doesn't. As I'm in no position to examine the evidence, I've asked Michelle to show it to Moira Reynolds in the hope that she may be able to make an identification. I don't know any small blonde thirty-year-old women. Do I?

*

Sally Lewis ate a little bit of dinner in the canteen. Not much, just a little. Hugh Davy's wife, Jenny, has gone back to Wales to look after their children, but Hugh has taken a week's leave from bus-driving and is visiting Sally every day. Her family have been coming in, too, and everybody looks tense but happy.

* * *

Today, I saw my young doctor again. He says I can go home. It might be six months before my cognitive behavioural therapy starts, but I'm to take the little yellow tablet for at least a year, anyhow. He says there's no rush to leave hospital – I can give it until the weekend.

I'm both glad and apprehensive. Hospital gives you permission to abandon your responsibilities and think about your own well-being. Out there in the world you have suddenly to function on all levels and in everyone's interests again.

When we had finished the medical business, my young doctor asked, sheepishly, whether I could, in fact, get my father to sign a copy of *Selected Poems 1965–1985* for him. This day was always coming.

* * *

I've tidied up my bed area in preparation for leaving. I've put all my old *Hey There!* magazines in the residents' lounge (which no one uses so why did I bother?). I've cleared my locker of biscuit wrappers and put my old newspapers into the pile for the recycling bin. Maura came over and said she was glad for my sake that I was getting better but that she'd miss me when I'd gone. I was touched.

Sally Lewis approached me and told me, bluntly but reasonably, that she doesn't want to have anything to do with the radio programme. Although it was as a result of it that she was reunited with her son, I don't blame her.

Cally stopped by my bed and told me that when she gets out she'd like to make me a rune, but she doesn't know where to send it. It seems to be an unwritten rule in here that we don't exchange addresses, so I asked her if she'd bring it to me in the Riverside shopping mall. I'm determined to go back. Cally said she would.

What is a rune?

*

Got a postcard from Lindy-May and Harry who are in Lanzarote and, according to the card, having a brilliant time. I didn't even know they were going away. Have they remembered they need to be back in time to open the summer fête?

*

Moira Reynolds came in to see me. She has viewed the CCTV footage of my car and has identified the UHT cream culprit. It is Mrs Ted Twome, wife of the mall's deputy manager. Moira asked me what on earth I'd done to upset her. I said I'd only set eyes on her once – in the staff canteen. Well, twice if you count that Thursday training morning when we'd lined up for the annual staff photo. Then I remembered that that was the day when I'd cursed myself for having bought an identical coral wrap-over top to the one Cheryl the PR girl had – it looked so much better on her than on me, and there we were in the same top in the same picture. Now I put two and two together. Mrs Twome must have had suspicions about Ted and someone called Cheryl, whom she'd heard about but didn't know. That day, she must have asked someone to point out which person Cheryl was, and they must have said, 'The one in the coral wrap-over top,' and her eye must have fallen on me instead of the real Cheryl. But, really! Little me have an affair with Ted Twome? It's too ridiculous! But apparently not to some . . .

Moira also told me that someone who has been asking after me all along and wanted to come and see me but didn't know if she'd be welcome was Janice the hairdresser. According to Moira, Janice had given me a tongue-lashing just before I'd become unwell, and she'd been very much regretting speaking to me like that, as she'd had time to think about it and knew she'd been out of order. I was so glad to hear this. I hate to be on bad terms with anyone. I'll go and see her once I'm discharged.

* * *

So. I'm home, and everyone has gone to school or work. I see the vacuum cleaner hasn't been out much in my absence. And the breakfast things have been cleared into the dishwasher, but the table hasn't been wiped. Perhaps I expected a little more fuss to have been made over my homecoming, but I, of all people, know how hard it is to find the time or motivation to make our gloomy house nice. Meanwhile, I'm feeling reasonably secure about the absence of vermin, although I can't completely shake off thoughts of that dreaded one per cent. However, my little yellow tablet may be going some way towards helping me cope.

There is a festering pile of new post to add to the old pile. I've picked through it and found two early Christmas-card catalogues, which I've perused over my morning coffee.

I tend to like the kind with greetings in seven international languages and images of children of the world holding hands. But all I can find are strange, elongated figures dressing strange, elongated Christmas trees, or Christmas baubles in the most un-Christmassy colours, such as coffee and cream. All this is described as 'contemporary Christmas', but it doesn't hit the spot for me.

*

The phone rang, but I didn't answer it. The caller left a message. It was kind-faced Caroline, secretary of our Parents' Committee. She wanted to double-check that Harry and Lindy-May are still coming to open the summer fête. I confess I'm a little worried about this too. What should I do?

*

I've rung Mark regarding the Lanzarote situation. He assured me that Lindy-May and Harry are due back tomorrow morning: Lindy-May first, at around breakfast time, and Harry a little later, as he's diverting to Edinburgh so that nosy-parkers won't see them flying in together and draw conclusions. They will arrive separately at school to open the fête at one o'clock. Phew. Mark also told me that *he* is taking the afternoon off from the magazine office to attend the fête. He practically never does anything like this, and I was so surprised that I told Mark so. Mark said that while I'd been in hospital he'd been talking to *him* about something that they wanted to run past me now, and that we could discuss it at the fête tomorrow. He didn't give me any clues about what it might be, and I was full of bright curiosity until I realised that the only thing it can be is that Mark is considering getting back with Tanya and wants to know what we think. I'd rather not be asked that one.

I also told Mark a little about what I'd been discussing with the doctor about perhaps having learned my anxiety, rather than inheriting it genetically. I wondered whether he could relate to that. It turns out that Mark and Lindy-May were adopted by their parents, so Mark can't say whether he has a genetic predisposition or not. However, he and Lindy-May are biological brother and sister, and while she spent all her time growing up outdoors with her non-anxious father and the horses, he was a lot closer to his musical, nervy mother. So, there you are.

*

I put the radio on but, of course, there was no Harry and no Lindy-May. Harry's show was being done by a younger man who played Shania Twain whereas Harry would have played Iris DeMent, and Lindy-May was stood in for by none other than Hilary, who played good tracks but lacked Lindy-May's warmth and sparkle.

* * *

What a day! And nothing went to plan. I should have guessed what was coming when I went to put on my preferred slimming white summer trousers, found they had a stain on them and had to wear my dumpy little blue jeans. But that was only the start. Perhaps foolishly, as I'm still on the fragile side of quite well, I took myself down to school at ten o'clock this morning to offer my help with setting up the fête. I was given a job folding tickets for the vast tombola, which featured Kathleen and Lorna's stuff from the mall, plus lots more donated items from mummies and daddies.

Just as my fingers were becoming numb, Caroline popped over to say that there was a call for me in the school secretary's office. I couldn't imagine who it might be. *Him?* To say he couldn't come, perhaps?

In fact, it was Mark Strain, and the news was not good. As in very not good. As in Lindy-May and Harry Ferris had got caught up in an airport strike, and they were stuck in Lanzarote.

I didn't pause for a minute to think how tired and emotional Lindy-May and Harry might be, how much of a strain it must be to be stranded like that, and Lindy in her condition. No. I thought only of our fête and the notice we had put in the paper promising the Zero FM celebrities and all the people we had told, and now it wasn't going to happen. I may have made a little moan into the telephone.

Mark had sounded really sorry to be the bearer of bad tidings. After a moment, he said, 'Look. It's a very long shot, but I only know one famous person other than my sister and her boyfriend. I can try and get him if you like.' I didn't ask who it was, though the only person to cross my mind was injured afternoon DJ Sandy Long, who is in the country but not yet back at work. He'd have to do. Anyone would have to do.

I then had to break the news to Caroline and the team. The air of disappointment was almost palpable. I'd set us up for this. I felt responsible. I told them Mark was trying to contact Sandy Long so at least we'd have somebody to do the honours, but I don't think they wanted him the way they'd wanted Harry, who spends his show flirting with callers and making them feel attractive. Sandy carries out stupid hoax calls and pranks that make people feel foolish.

*

After we'd got the tombola tickets done, we took a little tea break in the canteen kitchen, during which Mark rang again to say he'd been successful and we could relax in the knowledge that our fête would be officially opened, if not quite as advertised. He couldn't stay on and chat as, in the circumstances, he'd said he would go in his car, collect our VIP and bring him to school. Well, of course, with his injured leg Sandy Long wouldn't be able to drive himself. I told the others, who perked up enough to crack on and start assembling the gazebos.

*

Even though all our publicity stated that the fête would commence at one o'clock, we nevertheless found ourselves greeting a steady trickle of people from twelve thirty. We could actually hear them talking about Lindy-May and Harry Ferris and feared that we and Sandy would be met with an angry backlash when the change of plan was announced. We said nothing. At least the sun was beginning to break through, which was promising.

At twelve forty-five, I spotted him limping across the playground with his stick. I called, 'Sandy,' and hoped he would remember my forgettable face. He did. I tried to thank him for saving our bacon, but I couldn't get a word in edgeways. Sandy had one topic and one topic only in mind, and he was determined to talk about it: Sally Lewis. He had been the cub reporter who had told the story of the abandoned Baby Noel and had suspected all along that Sally Lewis was the baby's mother, but his editor had told him at the time he'd better not breathe a word of his suspicions. He wanted to know how it had finally come out. He wanted to know who Baby Noel had grown up to be. He wanted to get them on his radio show, ideally, but I told him the likelihood of that was nil.

I was trying to curtail his manic chatter and get him organised to do the official opening, but it was proving almost impossible. With just minutes to go before one o'clock, and with Caroline having appeared at my elbow in an effort to move us in the right direction, I finally barked Sandy down momentarily, only to discover that he had not been speaking to Mark Strain, and that he was not aware Lindy-May and Harry were delayed in Lanzarote, and that

271

he had dropped by to meet them by long-standing arrangement for a day out at an old-fashioned fête. Nobody had said anything to him about official openings . . .

And then, suddenly, everything went dead quiet. Not just with Sandy, but across the whole milling playground. I looked up and saw a pathway break open through the middle of the crowd, and a slow, rippling cheer rose, and the hairs on the back of my neck stood up as I saw Mark Strain walking through the cleared way, and beside him, no kidding, *no kidding*, Lorcan Hinds.

*

It turned out that Mark had met Lorcan Hinds at the races a couple of years ago, when he was famous but not *as* famous as he is now. Mark had given him a couple of tips, which had paid off handsomely, and they had returned to the races together a few times since. Most importantly for us, they had each other's mobile number.

If anything, Lorcan Hinds is more devastatingly handsome in the flesh than he is on telly. His hair is long, about chin-length, and expertly cut in layers to accentuate his prominent cheekbones. Don't ask me about his eyes. I could hardly bear to look. He also turned out to be a really good sport. He didn't just make a funny little off-the-cuff speech to open the fête, he went round the stalls taking a turn at helping. When Kathleen and Lorna arrived with Nathan and Samuel, he was working on the tombola, and when young Samuel's ticket won a prize, Lorcan Hinds presented him with it: a little old woman made up of a dish-mop, a dishcloth, a tea-towel and a duster. Lorcan Hinds even took a turn in the splash-the-teacher stocks, although how anyone could bear to throw a wet sponge at that perfect face I'll never know.

At about two o'clock, I was delighted to see Nurse Alison and Nurse Pat, in uniform, coming across the playground. The hospital is only a short walk from the school, and they had brought Maura, the smokers and Wilfred to the fête as a little outing. The smokers were looking particularly for the tombola to see what they could bag to bring back with them – until I told them that Lorcan Hinds was on the premises, at which point there was some gasping and whooping, except from Maura, who still prefers James Nesbitt, on account of his looking like her son, and Wilfred, who had never heard of Lorcan Hinds, or of *Mac*.

I met up with Mark in the tea tent and thanked him profusely for delivering such a star as Lorcan Hinds. He dismissed his part in it as unimportant, although he agreed it was quite a catch for the school. What with all the excitement, I'd forgotten that Mark had said he wanted to speak to me about something and only remembered when he appeared beside us, carrying a cup of coffee and a piece of fruit cake.

It was this. In the light of the new building in his village, Mark has decided to develop the steading where he has his antiques and collectibles business to add a gift shop and tea rooms. And he's offering it to us to run. Why us, I don't know. I suppose *he* has picked up a thing or two about managing small businesses, avoiding the pitfalls and so on from his years at the magazine. As for me, I've no credentials whatsoever! But Mark wants us to do it because he likes us, and his plan is to create a little sitting room at the back where the children can go after school and watch telly or do homework. Brian and Sheelagh will stand in for us six weeks in the year to provide us with holidays. And there will be a proper cook to do that side of things.

He is all on for it. He's keen to get out of the magazine and away from horrible Jeremy. He also likes the idea of playing *Mein Host* in a village tearoom and – it surprised me to learn – of seeing more of the children. I was a bit stunned, but I'll think about it, seriously.

I noticed that Mark's leather jacket was nowhere to be seen, and I was thrilled for him, though I passed no remark.

Later in the afternoon, who should turn up but high-fiving Michelle, with a little bit of gossip from the mall. Seemingly, young Penny Reynolds went on a post-exams holiday with 'the girls', and while she was away, Moira decided to redecorate her room as a surprise. However, it was Moira who got the surprise when she found the drawers under Penny's double bed stuffed with cosmetics and accessories that Moira hadn't given her the money to buy. Thus, Moira discovered that her daughter was a thief. She was absolutely furious and is making Penny take a job in an overall at the supermarket checkout until she has paid £500 to charity. Only then will she be allowed to keep what she earns!

After a bit, Lorcan Hinds came and joined us. He drank three cups of tea and ate four pieces of shortbread. (Not unlike Wilfred.) He also told us that it's going to be in tomorrow's papers that he's not the father of Beth Marsh's unborn baby and that the real father is an extra in Beth's latest project. Beth is returning to England to become the new district nurse in a regular Sunday-evening drama, and they're going to write her pregnancy into the storyline.

Eleanor and Terry popped up and were introduced, and it turns out that Lorcan Hinds is yet another fan of my father. He asked Terry if he was still writing, and Terry said he'd just destroyed a batch of rather bad poems, which had served to get him warmed up again. He was now intent on writing a short collection in tribute to Eleanor, whom he said he had only recently begun to appreciate as the heroic figure she actually is. Golly. Eleanor blushed!

At last, the fête was drawing to a close, and Lorcan Hinds, who must have signed about four million autographs, was called upon to fulfil one last task: the drawing of the raffle. Usually, I wouldn't even listen for things like raffle prizes, but when it's Lorcan Hinds talking, you pay attention to every word. And so I learned that I held the first-prize-winning ticket. I thought it was the barbecue – it's always a barbecue – but it wasn't. It was a hot-foam home car-wash machine. Good grief.

Acknowledgements

Thanks go to Faith O'Grady at the Lisa Richards Agency; my editor Ciara Considine and all at Hachette Books Ireland – Breda Purdue, Ciara Doorley, Ruth Shern and Peter McNulty; Hazel Orme; Róisín Ingle; and, as always and especially, to Robin and Myra, Niall, Keir, Clem and Nye.